I'M AN E.L.F.

Rava Watkins

Paperback ISBN 9798218505103
E-book ISBN 9798218505097

DEDICATION

E-**Encourage** daily; it builds faith and strengthens one's soul

L-**Love** mirrors one's self-image yet reflects God's radiance

F-**Forgive** as many times as infinity because infinity is boundless

~Do this always. Be an **ELF** every day~

PROLOGUE

Two weeks before Christmas. That part of the accident I remember so vividly because I begged my dad to drive us around to see the Christmas lights displays around town. My daddy piled us up in our Jeep and we headed down the country roads of Chattanooga. The night before was extremely cold and icy from the sleet that had fallen over. While Daddy turned on the heat to defrost the fog condensation on the windows, Mommy switched on the radio to play Christmas music. Oh, the sweet sound of Bing Crosby's *I'll Be Home for Christmas* illuminated the car speakers.

"Do you think they will play Christmas songs all night?" asked Mommy.

"I think they will. Man, this window is really fogging up!" said Daddy as he squinted his eyes at the window.

"I hope they play Christmas music, Daddy!" I said from the backseat.

"Babe, maybe you need to turn the AC on instead for just a bit," Mommy suggested.

My dad turned the wipers on to help clear a bit of the fog. I started singing my own jingle to *Jingle Bells*. My brother Chase was sitting in his car seat, being the terrible two he is. That's what my mom always said, wrestling with one of his toys. He dropped his dinosaur stuffed animal and began to whimper. I gazed out the window.

Mommy turned around to face him. "What's the matter?"

"He dropped his toy on the floor," I said.

"Aw, Chelsea will get it for you," Mommy said.

I looked down at the floor and saw that it was way on the other side of the seat. My dad was slowly driving up the ridge cut to head to the top of the ridge, the best Christmas lights displayed on the beautiful houses that sit on the ridge. While on the ridge, you have the best view because you can look over to the beautiful skyline of Chattanooga, Tennessee. I snuck a quick glimpse of view because I didn't want to miss it. Chase's whimpers turned into a full-blown holler from the top of his lungs.

"Hey, now stop that crying! Chelsea, did you get his toy?" asked Mommy.

I reached and stretched down to see if I could reach it. "Uh! Mommy, I can't reach it!" I said as I strained to get it. "It's way on the other side."

"Take your seatbelt off and just reach over to grab it." Mom directed. I unfastened my seatbelt and got down on the floor to grab it. I gave it to him while I playfully tickled him with the dinosaur. On the radio, *Santa Claus is Coming to Town*, sung by the Jackson 5, came on, and we all started singing with it.

"Wow, look at the lights over there!" Mommy said. "I think I will make a gingerbread theme somewhere in the house next year. Maybe the kitchen."

"That will be nice, babe. We'd have to start shopping early at Hobby Lobby, or Target may have some good deals." Daddy cut on the wipers to clear out the blurriness.

"Or maybe a Charlie Brown theme!" Mommy said. She turned around and looked at us with her beautiful smile.

"*What* the hell is he doing?!" Daddy peered through the window with confusion. "He's driving stupid!"

Mom jerked her head around to see what was going on. On the opposite side of the ridge was a truck swirling in and out of the lane to our lane. He was coming toward us at high speed.

"*Whoa!*" said Dad, "*Whoa!*"

"*Who-*" shrieked Mom.

The truck's high beams flashed upon us, quickly emerging toward our vehicle. Mommy quickly grabbed Daddy's arm. "*Babe-wait!*" Mommy squeaked out. The panic rushed from her voice into my ears. She screamed out as my daddy turned the wheel to avoid collision with the truck. We plummeted over the ridge. Our car flipped over and over and over down the steep terrain. My body flew up in the air, hitting every surface of the car. It all happened so fast. My head hit something hard, and I felt my body lift in the air as if I were floating into the night's stars.

Thump!

My head hit something hard, and my eyes drifted slightly from the stars to blackness. But the stars were no longer sparkling...there were spots of red.

I was confused.

Mommy! I want my mommy!

I looked over to see our car, and darkness embraced me.

CHAPTER 1

Ring.

"Hello, Callaway's Auto Repair Shop! How may we serve you?"

"Seth! I haven't heard from you in a long time! Is that you? How are you doing-how's the city life treating you?"

"Hey, Mr. Garrett!" I reached down the counter to pull out my dad's schedule book. I looked around to see if I could spot a pen. "Life is going okay at the moment. And you know me, just looking for the next story to publish." I didn't see a pen near me, so I walked to get one from my satchel. "And, of course, Atlanta's traffic will always be Atlanta's traffic."

Mr. Garrett laughed. "Just hang in there, a story will catch your eye soon. Is your dad around?"

"No, he's in the back tuning up my car. Do you need to talk with him?"

"No, just tell him that I will stop by tomorrow."

"Okay, Mr. Garrett, I will let him know."

"It was nice talking to you, son; hopefully, we can all go fishing one day."

"Yes sir, we'll have to do it one early Saturday morning."

I hung up the phone and placed the black book under the counter. I didn't put it as a schedule in the book because Mr. Garrett is a regular. My dad is Stephen Callaway. He's the owner of Callaway's Auto Repair Shop. It's been a family-owned business since the early 1950s when my grandfather Gregory Callaway first established it in Decatur, Georgia. It was a business that everyone knew about in the community of Decatur. People will come to get their cars looked over or get estimates. When people leave with their estimates, they will manage to come back for my dad to provide the service. I don't know if it was because my dad's prices were very reasonable for his service. Or because of his kind-hearted and thoughtful soul, he'd rather provide great service than no service at all.

Here I am. Seth Eugene Callaway, an editor from The Majestic, a magazine company based in Atlanta, Georgia. I'm the youngest of three siblings. Even though it is a family-owned business, I didn't want any part of it. I love my dad though. I love him immensely, but I don't want any part of the family business. Sometimes, I feel bad because I think my dad would prefer me to follow in his footsteps than my brother. But I didn't want to. Of course, when I'm around, I will help my dad out in any way that I can. My oldest brother and I had to help around the shop after our schoolwork, sometimes even before we went to school. We knew the ends and outs of the business because our dad taught us. He hoped we would change our minds one day, but for either of us, that day hasn't come yet. We each had our own separate lives right now. My brother Zachary isn't married but has two kids, Tiffany and William. He works at a factory that manufactures cleaning items for offices and stores- both domestically and internationally. Our sister, Cynthia Harris, is the middle sibling. She is married with three kids: Mariah, Luke, and Justin. Our mother, Kimberly Callaway, passed away when I was just about 10 years old. She had complications due to pneumonia and never recovered from it. I miss my mom. I hold on to every memory and every nostalgic feeling I had when she was alive.

I walked to the back of the shop, where my dad was finishing up on my car. He was closing the lid on my car when he looked up and saw me coming. Everyone says I resemble my dad the most out of my siblings. I can see some of my features in him, but I get my eyes from my mom.

"Mr. Garrett is going to drop by tomorrow to see you." I sat on one stool. "Y'all still hang out?"

"Whenever we can," He gave me my keys. "We catch a game here and there. Your car is ready to go. You're going to need an air filter soon. Just buy one and bring it to me." He picked up his coffee mug.

"Thanks, Dad." I looked at him. "Don't you ever get tired of doing this? I imagined you would have wanted something new by now."

"No, son, this is all that I have left now." He looked around the shop. "When your mom passed, this became like therapy for me. It's what helped me get by. This business took care of a lot of things...it took care of us."

He walked to the wall of pictures that he'd taken with us and with customers. I stood right next to him. There was a picture of my grandfather and dad standing in front of a repaired car. They both were smiling. The picture right beside it was a picture of Dad, me, Zach, and Cynthia smiling at the photographer.

Wow, I thought. Pictures can really tell stories. I was looking at the history of my family business.

Our history.

"Don't get me wrong, son. Sometimes I've wondered what life would have been if I didn't follow my dad's footsteps," he said.

And? I thought to myself.

"Then I realize life isn't bad at all." He chuckled and patted me on my back. "Besides, maybe you or Zach can take over, so I can retire. He walked to another car he had to repair.

Ugh! Not this again, I thought.

"Nope! Not me, Dad! Zach may be up to it. I got too much on my plate right now."

"Yeah, trying to find the next story huh?"

"You got it. I'm heading to the office to do some research. I will stop by Saturday to see you. Maybe we can catch a game or go fishing or something."

"Sure." He started coughing intensely. He took out his handkerchief to wipe his mouth and quickly placed it in his pocket. I went up to him, but he held his hand up.

"I'm okay. It's just a little cough."

"Are you sure, Dad? That cough sounded pretty bad."

"No, it's just my allergies. The weather is changing, so it's causing my allergies to flare up. I'm fine! I'm fine!" He sounded persistent in having me leave. "I'm all right."

"Okay, but I want you to follow-up with your physician, okay?" I ordered.

"I will". He assured me. He threw his hand up as if to brush me off and began working on another car.

I got in my car and peeled from the lot to head to the city.

***

There wasn't much traffic on the outskirts of the city as I drove into the parking garage to park my car. I got my ticket validated and walked down a couple of blocks to head into the office. It was very chilly outside. It was the start of the Fall Season. The Majestic is located right in the metropolitan area of Atlanta. It's a huge building; one of the top magazine publishing companies in the Southern region. The magazine covers many topics, from the latest trends, fashion & beauty, celebrity news, hot topics, and more. This magazine company is one that can literally make you or break you. You can make it by climbing up the top and running over anyone that gets in your way. You have to change your persona about everything. You lose your identity. More ass-kissing. More lies. More manipulations. More scandals. More complications. More stress. When you think you actually made it actually-you're still not officially there on top because there's always someone higher. It's good for a while until it's not.

When it breaks you, you feel like a failure. Nothing feels good anymore, and your mood is equivalent to your workload. You find yourself being complacent with the security of a job that you're no longer happy with. You're just there for the moment. Then here comes the question: Should I go? Should I stay? Should I say something? And if I do, will that change anything? These questions are usually answered by you leaving the company, termination, staying because you've invested so much, or unwilling to leave because of fear. Fear can also be substituted by a lack of faith.

Seth Calloway was neither of the two. I just wanted to make it. I've been working for this company since I graduated from grad school. I started out as an associate and then went to assistant editor, and now editor. My goal was to become a publisher. I pulled out my badge to swipe the scanner to gain access to the building. It was around 7:30 in the evening; mostly, everyone was gone from their shift. There were still some associates left who were finishing up on things that they were tending to. I took the elevator and went to the fourth floor, where my office was located. My office space wasn't very big. It had a couple of pictures of my family and pictures of columns that I wrote in the magazine. I placed my satchel on my desk, plopped down on the chair, and turned on my computer. I was in charge of the magazine's Ask Us Anything column. I have to hear what our fans, subscribers, bloggers, and social media content have to say. I also have to meet with the other magazine editors to finalize all content and images and get them ready for the next monthly issue.

I was reading my emails when my buddy JP walked into my office. JP was a very close friend, whom I met when we were just undergrads together. He is one of the art directors here with the company. We both started here as associates but later ventured into our own career path. He was a medium-built, stocky guy with a darker shade of skin. He was a funny guy. When we hung out with our friends, he was the one who kept us laughing and hyped up. I can talk to this guy about anything. He is married and has two little boys.

"Hey, I didn't know you were coming in today," he said as he sat in one of the seats in front of my desk.

"Yeah, I have a lot of things to catch up on man. I'm a little bit behind on the deadline."

"Have you found a story yet? You know Mrs. Decker is still in her office. She was making her rounds all day today." His eyebrows arched.

"Yeah-well..." I rubbed my head and narrowed my eyes to the screen. "...I just need a little more time."

"Did your dad get your car fixed?"

"Yeah, just needed a little tune-up." I stopped clicking the mouse on my computer and sat back in my chair. JP is a talker. "How's Lizzy and the kids?"

"Everyone is fine, man; the boys are digging more into inflation."

I chuckled. "Yeah, that's what happens when you have children in the house. And a big teddy bear to go with it."

JP chuckled. "Whatever man." He stood up. "You know I have to eat. I can't work off an empty stomach."

"We know!" I laughed with him, just by him mentioning having to eat. I haven't eaten anything all day. I was completely famished.

"You know we missed you at Juke Joint yesterday. Everyone was there."

"I know. I had to catch up on work." I stretched my arms out and yawned. I haven't been getting much sleep either. "Everyone was there?"

"Yeah, man...Kristy showed up too."

We usually get together as a group and do outings. We usually are about 6 to 8 of us in total. It started out as college roommates hanging out with our significant others. Then a couple of our coworkers were added to the group as well. Kristy was just a friend of a co-worker, Mia, but eventually became one of the groupies. I felt it was intentional because I was usually the odd man out. Everyone usually had someone except for me. I just casually dated. One thing led to another, and we all just started hanging out together. I found out Kristy was interested in me, and we went on a few dates. It was nothing serious. Kristy was a very attractive lady. She had a body to die for, and she was the top executive management for a business firm. I just wasn't feeling her. I didn't have that connection with her as she had with me. There was nothing there for me. That's part of the reason why I try to avoid the group setting. I nodded. "Yeah," I whispered to myself.

I went back to checking my emails on the computer. JP didn't want to press on the subject, seeing that I didn't want to convey the topic anymore, so he diverted my attention to something more positive.

"You spend so much time on work. You need to go out and live a bit." He walked back to my desk. "Maybe if you live a bit, then you'll find your story."

"What are you talking about? I do live." I said. I looked at him and sat back in my chair. I folded my arms across my chest.

"No, you don't, man; all you do is work. I'm talking about something you don't usually do-like sculpting, hunting, painting, anything to take you out the norm."

He had a point, I thought. I spend so much time with work or just doing the normal things that I do that I don't do things outside my box or out of my norm.

Do I live only for what's comfortable for me?

Have a reached the point where I'm just completely set in my ways? Do I only live only in the moment, not beyond?

Wow!

That hit me pretty hard.

I just sat there, marinating in my very thoughts.

"Are you okay, man?" JP asked. "I wasn't trying to scare you."

I chuckled to myself, "No, you're right; maybe I need to start doing things outside my norm."

JP still looked puzzled, "I'll leave you with your thoughts. I will holla at you later."

"All right man."

Just when he was about to walk out the door, Mrs. Olivia Decker strutted her way inside my office. She looked at JP, who politely smiled and quietly closed the door behind him. Then she cast me her usual look -no questions or comments just cut to the chase. She had long, straight, brunette hair that came right past her shoulders. She was tall and slender. Her make-up and pedicure were always on point. Every layer of her clothing was always drycleaned, ironed crispy, no lent, and very polished. She may have been in her sixties, but she looks well enough in her forties. She was the chief executive of The Majestic magazine. You never come to her, she comes to you.

"Simeon said that you were sending in some marketing ads to go with next month's issue." She looked at her nails and flicked them together. "I take it you do have everything in order for next month's issue."

"Yes. It will be ready by next week. I've helped Simeon before in marketing ads, and they were deemed successful." I had to put it out there since she was coming at me indirectly, suggesting I wasn't capable of taking on extra work. It's funny when it comes to a successful hive, it's the worker bees that build the strong colony.

"Great!" She turned around to walk to the door. "I know you won't disappoint me, Seth."

"Excuse me, Mrs. Decker, I want to talk to you about something." I stood up from my desk and went to approach her. "I wanted to see if it was ok for me to have my own individual column in the magazine to talk about area events and news. I feel the magazine should go more for personal experiences than commercial e-"

"Yes, that sounds great," She interrupted, "Maybe we can look into it. Please send an email, dear." She turned around and strutted out of the office.

I shook my head. I stopped sending emails to Mrs. Decker a while ago. The only response she gives me is a thank you or no response at all. I went back to my computer and typed in the word art studios in the search field. I think it is time to take myself out of the norm.

CHAPTER 2

The World of Art was displayed at the top of an old vintage, gray building. It was located on 11th Street near the Music Museum. I called and spoke with Mr. Scott Chaplin, who said that I could just come in to see how I would like it. I think this will be a fun experience to dive my hand into. I've taken art classes before in high school. I can draw pretty well. I think this will definitely help keep my mind off work. I just hope that I will like it. I step inside the building. The scents of wood and paint caress under my nostrils. On the walls were paintings displayed like a gallery. Beautiful paintings! I walked quietly down the hallway, observing every piece of painting. The hallway stretched to a door at the far end.

This is it.

No turning back.

I turned the doorknob. Inside was wide and open. It had a natural, earthly blend with natural white lighting that glistened in every corner of the room. There were two seats to every desk and eight desks in total. I counted nine students in the class, I would be the tenth. There was a man standing, who was leaning over talking to one of the students, then noticed me. He was an older man, very well-shaven. He walked towards me.

"Hello, you must be Seth Callahan?" the man asked. He reached out to shake my hand.

"It's Callaway." I politely corrected as I shook his hand.

"Oh-I'm sorry! I easily mix names up a bit. Welcome to The World of Art; I'm Mr. Scott Chaplin, the art director here." he introduced. "Please take any seat you like. Your easel, brushes, and color palettes are right before you."

"Thank you," I replied. I didn't know if he was from England, but his voice sort of had a bit of the accent.

"I will be walking around if you should need any help. You can paint whatever you like, or you can use the display piece set before you."

He smiled and walked away. He was a very friendly individual.

I looked around the room to see where I could sit when something, or should I say someone, caught my eye. Oh, my, she was very pretty! She sat there illuminated by this glow that only I could see. I walked to her desk. The closer I came, this raw emotion crept inside me. Her paintbrush went up and down. Up and down. I was a bit nervous when I sat in my seat. I took a glimpse of her, and she didn't once look at me. Her brush continued to stroke up and down. I decided to strike up a bit of conversation.

I glanced up to see the display of the painting in front of the classroom. It was a picture of a sunset over a beach. I looked at her easel. She wasn't painting the display in front; she was painting a garden of flowers. I lifted my brush and dipped it in the orange paint.

"Your painting is very beautiful," I said.

"Thank you," she said softly.

"My name is Seth. This is my first day here in class." I turned to look at her.

She only looked at the painting. Her skin was a creamy, smooth caramel. She had a nice, athlete built. Not too slim, just a little thickness. Her eyes were beautifully dark and dramatic.

"How long have you been painting here?" I asked.

"I've been painting here for about three years, but I started painting when I was eight."

"Well, you're very good at it."

"Thank you. How long have you been painting?" She asked me.

"Just today. I wanted to take my hand in something new."

"Good choice. The hand is a great tool to use for painting and sculpting. Mr. Chaplin taught us that."

"May I ask you what your name is?"

"Chelsea." Softly.

"Well Chelsea, I think I'm going to like this class."

She smiled and continued to paint.

The rest of the time in the classroom was pretty quiet. Out of the corner of my eye, I watched her paint. Sometimes as she paints, she would hum a tune. I couldn't make out the tune, so I couldn't hum it with her. But I thought, best not. I didn't want to try so hard. Of the amount of conversation that we had, I realized I had to go steady with her.

"You're doing well, Mr. Calloway," Mr. Chaplin was standing right beside me. "How did you enjoy your first day?"

"I enjoyed it very much. I had a great time."

"We hope to see you again."

I smiled and nodded.

He walked over to Chelsea, placed his hands over her shoulders, and said, "Exquisite!"

"Thank you, Mr. Chaplin," she responded.

Mr. Chaplin walked to the front of the class.

"May I have your attention? Class will be ending here shortly. If you choose, you can take your portraits with you or leave them here to dry. You can stop by later in the week to pick them up. As I say every section, art can truly define and express who you are as an individual. Leave here and be creative."

That was some really great advice, I thought to myself. I looked around the room and everyone was gathering their belongings to get ready to leave. I turned to Chelsea; she had left her portrait on the table and was heading out of the classroom. I quickly gathered my satchel, placed it over my neck, and grabbed my painting. I rushed out of the classroom to catch up with her. When I saw her, I saw a long cane stretched out from her hand, tapping the floor as she moved. I didn't realize it. She was blind.

Chelsea *was* blind!

And I was speechless.

My heart pricked just a bit. There she was, a girl who's fragile and vulnerable to the outside world, even those who are around her, is in an art studio painting. Yet, I felt completely drawn to her.

Infatuated and intrigued. I couldn't explain it, but I was.

I ran up to her.

"Hello, Chelsea! I wanted to stop you; you left your painting behind."

Her expession seemed surprised that I approached her.

"It's okay. I tend to always leave my paintings behind. I always come back for more sessions. I can use the extra credit."

She laughed at her own joke. I laughed right along with her. "If anything, *I* need the extra credit."

She chuckled to herself. Everyone walked past us as they were leaving the building.

"Um, do you need a ride home? I know you just met me, but I don't want you out here by yourself."

"Thanks, that's very sweet. I have someone coming to get me. She's running just a bit late. Besides, Mr. Chaplin can take me home if she's not able to. Thanks anyway."

"Ok, well I'll keep you company until she arrives. Plus, my dad always told me to make sure a woman is taken care of way before you. So, I will wait if that's ok."

She chuckled again. "It's ok."

"So, are you originally from here?" I asked.

"No, not really. I'm from Chattanooga, Tennessee, but moved here when I was six."

"I don't think I've been to Chattanooga before. I've heard it's really nice."

"It is! It's home. Chattanooga is a very beautiful city with people, food, and scenery! I really miss it at times! I love it here as well. I wouldn't change anything. Well, maybe *one* thing..."

She lowered her head a moment. Being blind was still a soft spot for her. Maybe she hasn't gotten over not having her sight.

"Well," I began to say when the door swung open.

"Chelsea?!" a voice said.

"Tamara!" Chelsea replied.

"Sorry I'm late, are you ready to go?" Tamara reaches out and gently grabs Chelsea's arm.

"Yes." She turned to my direction. "Thanks for staying with me."

Tamara looks back and forth from me to Chelsea.

I extended my hand. 'I'm Seth, I waited with her until you came." She shook it.

"I'm Tamara, her cousin, thank you," she nudges on Chelsea's arm. "We have to go now."

Chelsea nodded. She was hesitant at first, then walked to their car, which was parked right in front of the building. I watched as they got in the car and drove away. Then, like gravy to biscuits, it *hit* me!

JP was right! I found my story. Chelsea *was* my story.

***

We were heading toward home, Tamara's house. Tamara Cook is my cousin. Well, we're very close, so it's almost as if we were sisters instead of cousins. After the accident, my dad's sister brought me here to stay with them. When Tamara graduated from college, she got married and moved into a house in Alpharetta, Georgia. Tamara moved me in with her. She said her mom, my Aunt Linda, was set in her ways and I wouldn't be as happy. I would have to say my family came through even though I know it wasn't easy on them or me. Especially for me because I did lose everything. I lost my family and my sight. I still haven't coped with the trauma that I endured as a child. Sometimes, I feel as if I'm a burden to them and to myself.

"Seth seems like a pretty nice guy. Is he new to the class?" Tamara asked.

"Yes, he started today."

"It seems as if he might have a little *thing* for ya."

"I don't know about that. I think he's nice to everyone." I didn't want to continue this conversation about Seth. This was *really* bad news. Falling in love or any hint of intimacy can be challenging for anyone, especially worse for a blind person. I've been through so much; I don't want to be hurt again.

I can feel the silence. I'm sure Tamara may have been looking at me.

"You know it's okay to have a friend, right? Maybe God is trying to show you something."

"Whatever is *shown,* I can't *see* it!" I turned to Tamara's direction, "I'm blind *remember?*"

"Just give him a chance, ok? You just never know," she assured me.

We rode in silence all the way to her house.

Once we arrived, Tamara got out to help me out the door. "So, how does he look?" I asked.

"He's very attractive in a rustic Southern type of way."

We laughed.

"He's tall and slender. He has a pretty smile. He seems like a cool decent guy."

"Yes, I love how he talks. His voice is very smooth and calm. Very poetic."

She led me into the house. Tamara works from home. She is an HR rep for a medical insurance company. She can work anywhere as long as she has her laptop with her. This is very convenient for me, because I may have things that I have to do or places I have to go. Ha! The only places I usually go is the art studio or to the blind school to put in volunteer hours. I'm pretty much for the most part at home. Tamara stays in a two-story leveled house, so I had to quickly adjust to going up and down stairs. I don't mind at all. Aunt Linda was a single-level home, and I shared a room with Tamara. At Tamara's house, I have my own bedroom. I have a big space that I use to paint and to store my paintings. Joseph, Tamara's husband, knocked down a wall so that I could have extra space. He's a nice man. He's part Black and Hispanic. Sometimes I hear him talk in Spanish and often times I hear him talk in English. He is a contractor and has his own construction company. They have a beautiful daughter Kyla, who I claim as my niece, but is actually my cousin. Sometimes, we paint together, or she helps set up my paint supplies in my room. Of course, sometimes I do get lonely. Joseph greeted us at the door.

"Hey babe," Tamara said.

I can hear his footsteps walk over and I heard the sound of a kiss.

Here comes loneliness, I thought to myself.

"Mommy, Mommy!" screamed Kyla. I could hear her little footsteps tap quickly against the floor, so I knew she was running. Kyla always be running around the house. "Hey, Aunt Chel!" That was her nickname for me.

"Hey, Kyla."

"I'm going to get dinner started," Tamara said.

"Ok, I'm going to lie down a bit. I'm a little tired."

I reach my stick out to guide me to the stairs. From that point on, I knew where to go. As I went up the stairs, I heard the sweet sounds of laughter, giggles, and love. I close the door behind me and lay on my bed. Yearning for the sounds I would hear if I had my own home and family.

My husband will come home from work and tell me all about his day. Then, if I'm tending to the garden or keeping up the home, he will be playing with the kids until he gets tired. We will make sure that the kids get their homework, studying, and practicing done for all activities. When I'm in the kitchen, making a meal, he will be right there helping me blend it altogether. Or at least telling me everything smells delicious. Afterward, we will get them ready for bed, study the Bible, read books, and pray. We will hug, plant kisses, and sing them right to sleep. The last couple hours of the night will be *our time.* Our time to relax, be adventurous, create new things, be intimate, bond, and love each other. Before we go to sleep, we will pray together to build a close relationship with God.

I think about those moments all the time.

Almost every day.

Oh, what a beautiful bliss!

Then I thought about Seth.

CHAPTER 3

I parked outside the art studio. I wanted to catch him first thing in the morning before a session started. I know he would have insight on what made Chelsea so gifted with her artwork. I just hope he wouldn't object to me asking questions, being that I just met him yesterday.

Well, here's goes nothing, I thought to myself.

I pushed the door open and walked in. He was nowhere in the front space, so I proceeded down the hall to the studio room. From the doorway, Mr. Chaplin was on the far side of the room, roaming through art displays.

I cleared my throat.

"Mr. Chaplin."

He turned around.

"Ah, Mr. Calloway. Did you want to pick up your portrait?"

"Oh, no, I took it home with me yesterday." He looked puzzled.

"Oh, well, you know sections don't start until a couple of hours."

"Well, I didn't come for a session, Mr. Chaplin. I actually came to talk to you. I was wondering if you could answer some questions for me."

"Sure, what kind of questions?"

"Well, you see, I'm a journalist-well editor, but I still do a lot of writing, so I still do journalist type of work. I work for *The Majestic,* it's a magazine company."

'Oh yeah! I've heard of it," He sounded more pleased then. "I've read some of your magazines. I must say I've never had a journalist come to my studio before in the five years I've been here. I'm very intrigued by that."

"Yes, well I wanted to ask you just a few questions about a student."

"Ah, could that be a Miss Chelsea Davis." He smiled. "I noticed you've never finished your portrait because you were too busy gawking at her."

I laughed. "Yes well-

"What is it that you want to know?" he sounded very curious. "Could it be that you want to know where she gets her remarkable talent?"

"Yes, that's one of my questions."

"Well Mr. Calloway, that's a question you will have to simply ask her. Art can naturally be a person's ability...skill...and Mrs. Davis possesses *both* of each. She only paints what she sees. She uses all her senses and puts it all into a painting."

"Has she ever told you what made her start painting in the first place? Was it passed down from a family member?"

"Don't insult *art,* Mr. Callaway. Everyone has a bit of art rooted deep inside them. The very creation of this world is art...the psalms of David is art... the songs derived from Solomon is art...*art* is everywhere Mr. Calloway. Miss Davis came to this very studio three years ago with an extraordinary gift. Some of which are hung upon this very studio."

"Have you had buyers come by to purchase her paintings?"

"Of course...but they're not for sale until Miss Davis deems so. But... until then Mr. Callaway...let her paint." He smiled at me.

I nodded.

He walks back to resuming what he was doing when I first came in. I went down the hall to snap pictures of the portraits on my phone. I also snapped pictures that were displayed in the front area space. I tried to do it quickly without Mr. Chaplin finding out. I left the studio. Mr. Chaplin had to come from some part of England. His voice, mannerisms, and demeanor all point to it. I could see Mr. Chaplin in a Shakespearean play or at the lounge reading poetry. I did learn that he does have a keen admiration for her work and respects her gift as an artist. So do I to some extent. But why hide your work? Why does Chelsea have art as a keepsake? I have to find the answers.

***

I walked into class, and I had this inkling feeling that Seth was there. Part of me hoped that he would be. I asked myself what harm could come from just talking to someone.

Nothing.

Just casual conversation.

I walked to my seat, and I smelled his presence. He's *here*. It was the same aroma I smelled last time we were here. My nerves started to build up.

"Hi there!" he said to me.

"Hello."

"I'm glad to see you made it today. You look very pretty."

"Thanks." See, now I *know* he's full out. I just threw on a pair of jeans and a T-shirt that I'm sure is highly loose with wrinkles.

"What picture is showing on display for us?" I asked him.

"It's a picture of apple orchards. I guess it's a kick toward the Fall season, huh?"

"I actually like the fall season, the blend of colors and the crisp air. The aroma of smells- speaking of smells," I turned towards him, "you must love peppermint."

He laughed, "My dad always had complimentary peppermint candy in a huge bowl for customers to grab at his shop."

"Shop?"

"Yes, my dad works on cars. He repairs them. He has his own shop in Decatur. It's a family-owned business. So what else can you smell on me?"

"I don't know-you have this scent. It's a blend of peppermint-

"Calvin Klein," he interjected.

"I guess...it has a bit of spice in it as well. You smell very distinctive."

"I'm glad that my scent doesn't frighten you, or that you frown your nose up every time you see me because I smell."

I laughed.

"No, it's quite a distraction, in a good way."

"Oh, well that sounds good! I don't want to distract you off your game. Instead of apples, you'll be making lemons!"

I laughed, "Shut up." Then I began to work on my portrait.

"How do you know what color to use when you paint?" he asked.

"Mr. Chaplin places my color palette the same every time I come. Some dark color oil paints have a stronger smell compared to the light color paints. Then I just go with the stroke of the brush. I paint on how I feel, how people feel, what the world looks like, or what I *think* the world should look like. Painting makes me feel alive-it's what keeps me going."

"You're very good at it. Don't ever stop painting. I'm an editor for a magazine. I can use some of your paintings to go in one of my magazine articles. I'm sure people would love to see that!"

"No! I just don't think people will understand." I shook my head. Bad idea. If he placed my paintings out there then that will mean exposure and vulnerability to the world that I'm not ready for. Sometimes the world can be cruel and harsh to those who are crippled or disabled. I felt his hand gently touch my arm.

"You can help them to understand."

A touch of warmth inside echoed throughout my body. It was something calm and promising the way he said it. My heart skipped a beat.

Mr. Chaplin was making his rounds. I heard the sound of his leather shoe stopping by our desk to show Seth how to make his trees look more real. I laughed when Mr. Chaplin said that his trees look like paintings from a five-year-old.

"You talk about your dad a lot. Are you the only child?"

"No, we are really close though. I have an older brother and sister. My mom passed away when I was ten years old."

"I'm sorry to hear that." I wanted to reach out and grab him in my arms, but I refrained from doing it. I can hear the sadness in his voice.

"Yes, I miss her. That's why I'm close to my dad. I didn't want him to hurt. He was a single father raising three kids. I just wanted to keep his spirits lifted. I try not to think about it as much. I cry sometimes. Then I work and keep going. Are you close with your parents?"

"No, well I used to be." She responded quietly.

It was a subject that I never talked with to anyone besides family. I didn't want to rehash that event that cost me my sight. That cost me my family. I think Seth got the message because he didn't ask any questions about my parents beyond that.

"Hey, I was wondering if you weren't busy this Friday, maybe we can grab a bite to eat? I know this place that has a really nice vibe."

"I don't know."

"Come on Chelsie. I like you, and I want to take you somewhere that's beyond your world of art."

I laughed. He has quite a way of making me laugh. How could I say no.

"Ok, I will go."

"Ok."

For the rest of the session, we just cut up and laughed. He told me about his childhood experiences and the customers he encountered at his dad's shop. I just let him talk the session away. He talked about his job. I was getting the feeling that maybe he needs to start his own adventure from his workplace. He said that he liked my picture, and I told him he could keep it. So, he took my picture home. After the session, we exchanged numbers, and I gave him Tamara's address for him to pick me up. He talked to Tamara a bit before we headed off down the road.

***

31

I had a date night, and I was super ready. I was very nervous. I've never actually been on a date before. My eyes welled with tears because this is my very first date and my mom or dad isn't here to see me off. My dad can't tell him what time he needs to bring me home, even though I'm well beyond my thirties. My mom isn't here to do my make-up and hair, or just to tell me how beautiful I looked. Luckily, I have Tamara who is very good at making sure I am on point from head to toe. It still isn't the same though. A lot of times, we think more about the people who are not physically with us, instead of appreciating the people who are with us. The people who help fill the void in our lives. Moreover, I think they would've been proud of me. I think they would have liked Seth as well.

I was standing in the living room waiting for Seth. Joseph, Tamara, and Kyla were all super excited for me. I had on a long, silky black dress with silver sequin flowing from top to bottom of the dress. Tamara let me borrow her black shawl to cover over it because it was a bit nippy outside. I had on some black, three-inch heels to go with it. My hair is natural, so Tamara clipped all my hair to one side, so it can hang over to one side. I also borrowed Tamara's black purse to set off the whole attire. Kyla said I looked very pretty. So, I believed her.

There was a knock on the door, Joseph went to open it. His scent captured my nose.

"Hello, I'm Seth."

"Hello man, I'm Joseph, you know Tamara, and this is Kyla. Come on in."

"Hello!" said Kyla. "Are you taking my aunt out on a date?"

"Kylie!" Tamara called.

"Yes, I am.... wow!" his breath caught him. "You look beautiful Chelsea."

"Thank you."

I felt his footsteps come toward me. He took my arm with his and guided me to the door.

"Wait before we go, let me grab my rod." I was about to walk to grab it when he pulled me back to him.

"You're not going to need it tonight. Are you ready to go?" I nodded.

"Y'all have fun!" squealed Kyla.

He guided me outside the door. I'm sure Joseph, Tamara, and Kyla were smiling from ear to ear.

"Ok there's one step, two steps, three steps," he said.

I've counted the steps over a million times, but it was so cute that he was guiding me down the stairs. So, I didn't say anything.

I just let him lead and I followed.

We headed into town. Of course, I didn't know where we were exactly going because he wanted it to be a surprise for me. I did know that we fell upon some traffic, but of course, that is not typical here or anywhere else for that matter. I didn't know what he was wearing, but I could tell it was something very silk. I remember the feel of my dad's shirts when he would take Mom out.

"Are you excited about tonight?" he asked me.

"Yeah." I didn't mean for my response to sound a little unsure. I was still a bit nervous and overwhelmed at the same time. This was a new experience for me, and I had a bit of fear and excitement all within the same level. I just hope it wasn't viably transparent for him to see by the responses to his questions.

"You are going to enjoy yourself. Have you been to a bar before with live music or poetry reading?"

"No this is the first for me. I usually don't go out and have fun like that."

"*Really?!* Well, we're just going to have to change that."

What seemed like hours turned into minutes pretty quickly. The next thing I knew, he helped me out of the car. I heard him toss his keys to someone who offered to park the car. "Thanks, man," was what I heard him say. I can hear the music blazing from the outside. It sided like a bit of Jazz. I heard someone in passing say either the *Crystal Lounge* or *Cat Lounge* as we were approaching. I had my arm locked around his arm, his hand closed in on mine. It seemed as if we were walking a bit of a stretch before Seth stopped. He opened the door, and the aroma of food hit my nose. It smelled so good.

"Ok, let's go in."

I was hesitant for just a bit. Then he walked closely to me. I felt his chest on my shoulder, and he whispered softly in my ear. "You have to trust me. I won't let anything happen to you."

Then, I thought I felt his lips pressed up against my ear and my knees weakened a bit. I felt almost empowered to reach up, grab his head, and kiss him passionately. I couldn't explain this overlap of emotions that beckoned inside me when all I got was just a whisper from him.

"Ok, I don't know what causes me to do that. Sometimes I feel as though my legs get off balance sometimes." I replied.

"It's ok, I got you."

We walked inside the building. I heard a guy greet us by the door. I heard Callaway mention his name and said that he had reservations for the VIP. He guided me along what seemed to be a ramp before we got to our seats. He slid the chair behind my legs to help me sit down.

"What do you think so far?"

"I think it's really nice. The food smells great, and I love the music. It has a cozy feel."

"Yes, that's one of the reasons why I come here so much. I just can't keep away."

"Do you bring your dates here often?" I asked him.

"No, not often. And that's because I rarely go out on dates. So, if I bring someone out here, then that means that you're special."

"I've never been to a place like this before"

"It won't be your last."

I heard footsteps approaching us.

"Are you ready to order?" a voice asked. "I can start you off with drinks."

"I will have a sweet tea."

"I will have the same and also a cup of water," I said to the waitress.

"Ok, I will bring it out to you," the waitress turned and walked away.

"What are you going to order? I'm sure they don't have a menu in Braille."

He laughed.

"They have great seafood! I think I will go for the shrimp Cajun pasta and an order of their calamari. It's fire!"

"Ok, I will have the same."

"Um, I don't know if you can handle the spice. It's not for the faint heart."

I laughed. "Whatever, I can handle it!" I paused a moment to gather everything around me. "Tell me what you see. I always asked people to describe any area so I can get a visual of it."

He grabbed my hands to set them on the table so that I could feel the table. It was round. He placed my hand on the fork, spoon, knife, and napkin that was placed in front of me.

"There's a row of tables and chairs on the level and on the bottom. In the center, there is a small dance floor. There's a stage where a band is playing some soft music. There's a bar off to the left of the stage. The kitchen is in the back. The inside is a fiery red with gold trimming. Hey- do you want to dance?"

I shook my head. "No!"

Seth grabbed my hand. "Have you ever danced before?"

"No-not being blind!"

"Come on. I'll show you."

He lifted me up from the seat and walked me to the dance floor. I felt the change from the soft carpet to something hard right underneath me. The music was louder on the floor than in our seats.

"People will be looking at me," I said.

"Yes, because you're pretty. They will be looking at me because I can't dance." He said over the music. "Who cares?! Maybe we can teach them something!"

He wrapped his arms around my waist and pulled me closer to him. I couldn't help but to laugh and blush. I wrapped my arms around his neck and began to sway to the music. It was an upbeat song. I couldn't help but find my rhythm and just go with it. Then memories of my mom dancing with my dad resurfaced in my mind. I let go of his neck and snapped my fingers in the air as I swayed to the music. I was in the moment, and it felt so real. I just kept smiling and smiling. I surprised myself with my moves and I *know* I surprised Seth. The music slowed down to a slow jam. He pulled me up against him. I laid my head on his chest. He rested his head on me. I wanted the music to take me away with him. I just wanted to dance all night.

The rest of the night, we ate our delicious food and sipped on some wine. I didn't like the wine being it was my first time drinking it. But I did enjoy the tropical margarita. We laughed and enjoyed each other's company. We listen to a couple of people who read some poetry. It was beautiful. The vibe was amazing. I can do this spot any day of the week. After it was done, he took me home.

"Thank you, Seth. I had a great time tonight. You took me out on my first date." I held onto his arm as he guided me up the stairs.

"I feel special. Now I created a fun memory for you. I hope there will plenty more. You're not a bad dancer either. It was hard keeping up with you."

" *What*ever," I laughed.

"Tomorrow, do you want to hang out or do something?"

"Sure!"

"Ok, I will pick you up, and maybe we can go on a picnic somewhere."

"Ok, but I will bring the food."

"Deal!"

He leaned over and he wrapped his arm around me to give me a hug. I quickly reach out my hand to feel over his entire face. He touches my hand and the warmth inside heated every inch of me.

He guided my hand all over his face.

"You're beautiful too," I told him.

Then I felt his hand on my face, and he pulled me to his lips. I opened my mouth for him to gain entrance. His slick tongue was caressing mine. His lips were smooth and wet. I lost myself completely within his kiss. I *couldn't be*-lieve this was my first kiss!

I could kiss him all night, and I wanted to. It was something I never felt before and it frightened me. I broke away from the kiss.

"I have to go inside." I knocked on the door.

"Ok."

Joseph opened the door to let me in. "Bye Seth."

"Bye Chelsea."

CHAPTER 4

I pulled up in my dad's driveway. I felt bad that I hadn't come by to see him, nor did I come to take him on that fishing trip that we talked about when he worked on my car. So, I decided to pay him a visit. It was Saturday, so I knew he wasn't working on any cars today. He was probably in the living room watching a college game. I need to make sure he is okay from the last time I saw him when he was coughing profusely. I've been a bit busy with work and now Chelsea. Last night was amazing. But I realized she had a wall built up. I have to get her to trust me, so she can open up to me. There's something hidden in her that she hasn't shared. I will get the answer and share her story with the magazine, "a blind woman with an extraordinary talent"- who knew! She makes me wonder how there's so many gifted people in this world who keep their talents hidden. If you keep your talent hidden, then you'll not be able to bless the world. God uses us to bless each other. I know Chelsea isn't going to like it but I *have* to share her story.

I made my way to the house. The shop was a few blocks down the road. When we were younger, my siblings and I used to just walk to the shop and walk back home. The house was a single-level home with three bedrooms. The house hasn't changed since I left.

I was walking up the driveway when I heard a sound.

"Whoo-hoo!"

I turned around and it was Mrs. Jenkins. She's a sweet lady but the typical noisy old lady who knows about everyone in the whole neighborhood. But you better believe if something comes up missing, she will know the culprit.

I walk over to the side of the house. "Hello, Mrs. Jenkins! Do you need me to take the trash out?"

"No baby, I just wanted to talk to you a bit. Look at you, so handsome. I just wanted to let you know, your father doesn't seem to be doing well lately. I don't think he's been to work the last couple of days."

"Ok, Mrs. Jenkins, I'll go in and check on him." I turned to walk away. I didn't want to linger too long because Mrs. Jenkins could talk.

"You children all come by to see your dad more often and don't forget about me." She echoed behind.

"I won't, Mrs. Jenkins," I shouted back and waved my hand. I pulled out the key to unlock the door.

I walked inside and everything seemed in order. Nothing was out of place. "Hey Dad!" I called out and closed the door behind me.

No answer. "Dad!"

Dad came around the corner.

"Hey, son." He walked and gave me a hug. "I didn't know you were stopping by. I could have put on a pot of chili or something."

"No, you're fine Dad. I'm leaving to meet someone anyway to go on a picnic."

"Oh ok. Who is this new lady?"

"Her name is Chelsea. I met her at an art class I've been going to."

We headed to the living room. No wonder he didn't hear his name the first time. The game was on, and the volume was really turned up. I grabbed the remote to turn it back down some.

"So, am I going to meet this lucky lady soon?"

"I think so. I like her. There is one thing though um…she's blind." Dad looked up at me.

"Really?! I'm sorry son." he said to me.

I waved my hand, "Don't be sorry for me or her. I want to treat her as normal as she can be. She just lost her sight that's all."

"I wish your mom could see how great of a man you are."

"Hey, I have to give you some credit too." The phone started ringing.

"Dang! Where did I put that blasted phone?" He got off the chair and went to searching.

"I'll help you look for it."

Then he started coughing again. This time he bent over holding his belly as if he was about to vomit.

"Dad!"

I ran to him. He grabbed his handkerchief as he coughed and wiped his month. He quickly places the handkerchief in his pocket.

"I'm all right, I'm all right!" he shouted to me.

The phone stopped ringing. I turned him around and brought him back to the couch. "I thought you were going to get that checked on. What did the doctor say?"

"I ain't seeing no doctor, Seth! I'm fine! Leave well enough alone." The phone began to ring again. This time I got up.

"You sit there, and I'll find the phone." I began to walk when I abruptly stopped. I gazed down on the floor.

On the floor was a handkerchief that had bloodspots on it. I picked it up. I left the room to find the phone. I saw his cell phone on the kitchen counter and answered it.

"Hello…Oh what's up Zach…. yeah, I've only been here a few moments. I'm worried about him…he's coughing profusely…it means *a lot* Zach…he's not wanting to listen to me….

yes, he *is* being stubborn…well you and Cynthia need to intervene as well…yes, but I will be leaving shortly. Okay, see you soon." I hung up the phone and brought Dad his cell phone.

"You dropped this on the floor as well," I said and handed him the handkerchief of blood. He snatched it out of my hand. "Is this why you haven't been going to work?"

"Who said I haven't been going to work?"

"Mrs. Jenkins stopped me before I came in the house to tell me."

"That nosey old hag-"

"She's worried about you and so are we."

"I'm fine!" He shouted at me.

"No, you're not Dad and you're going to see a doctor before it gets worse."

I stayed a little while longer watching the game with him. He didn't want to talk about it anymore. He still was coughing here and there, but he didn't bother hiding the handkerchief since he got caught. Zachary came by with his girls and some wings. I stayed a little while longer before I left to meet Chelsea.

***

I brought Chelsea to Piedmont Park. It's a huge park. It was fall and the trees would be gorgeous around this time. The park is very romantic and secluded. I took her to this big tree with a pond right across the way. She let me guide her there; there were moments when she would hesitate, but then she would let me pull her through. I had my satchel with me, and I carried the basket in one hand. I lay the blanket on the ground and set the food on the blanket. She made cold-cut sandwiches, chips, potato salad, a container of assorted fruits, juices & water bottles, cookies, chocolates, paper plates, utensils, and napkins. I showed her when I placed each item on the blanket, so she would know. I also described the area so she could get a visual.

"Thanks for bringing the food. This looks really good." I told her.

"You're welcome. I hope you're hungry. I wanted to make sure you got enough."

"Oh, this is nice. All we're missing is candlelight."

She chuckled while eating a piece of fruit. "You really make me laugh Seth."

"I'm glad I make you laugh…there's a lot I don't know about you. Like what's your favorite color?"

"Red. What's yours?"

"Green…your favorite food?"

"Fries…and yours?"

"Wings. I love wings, especially if they're spicy…I know you love the fall season, but what's your favorite holiday?"

"Aw Seth, I absolutely love Christmas. I love everything about it."

I saw the gleam in her eyes. Her face reflected this glow. It was that moment of pure happiness in her voice about how she shared her love for Christmas.

"Tell me why."

"It's a beautiful holiday that represents love in so many ways: spiritually, emotionally, physically, and mentally. I feel it's the *only* holiday where we feel the most humble; in love, in giving, in songs, in worship, in sharing and caring, in faith. I love every crevice of Christmas. I love the lights, decorations, food, smells, stories, and family gatherings. I love Santa, Frosty, and the elves.

I laughed.

"Hey elves are the underdogs, but they do the most. They help, serve, and get the job done. I love elves! Hey, give me Christmas every day!"

"I hope I get to spend Christmas with you."

"We'll see….so Seth what do you like to do for fun?"

"Hey, I'm just about game for anything. My dad said that one day he would like to travel and visit some countries. I said I think I might just do that. I want to see the world for what it is. Then tell about it."

"You should. Go out there and explore."

"Would you come with me?"

"No, not the first round. Save me for the next round."

"Really?! You wouldn't want to go with me?"

"Nope. I feel everyone has their own journey that they should embark on. When you're on your own journey then you're vulnerable to accept God's hand. That's how you become closer to him. That's what my dad always said.

"Have you started your journey yet?" I asked her.

"No, not yet."

"Well, what are you waiting for?! You have this amazing gift you can open up your own art studio to showcase your paintings. Or teach an art class to other students who are blind and share the same gifts!"

"Well, what about you?! You can write your very own novel. Or you can invest in your own magazine company and see where that leads you!"

She was right. We both were. Was it fear that was holding us back? Or was it failure? Why do we sit around and waste our gifts?

Why do we allow opportunities to pass us by?

I asked myself these questions all the time. But I never answer them.

We sat on the blanket eating the rest of our food. I grabbed my satchel and pulled out the majestic magazine.

"Why do you always bring that bag?" she asked me. "I've felt it on your shoulders before, and the sound is familiar."

"I always bring it just in case I have a story a write." She found my shoulder and laid her head on it.

"When you write your first novel, I have dibs on the first published, but it must be in Braille though. That's another thing I love to do is read but I can only read Braille writing."

"I'll remember that. When the holidays come, I want you to paint me something festive."

She laughed. "I will."

A moment paused.

"Can I ask you a question?" I asked. "How did you lose your sight?"

I knew I was pushing it, but I had to know. I wanted to know.

I wanted her to open up to me.

"It was around Christmas. It's ironic because that's my favorite holiday. But I was about six years old. I wanted to see the lights, and I begged my dad so that we could go. It was a bit icy on the roads and my dad's mirror kept fogging up." She paused a moment as she looked out toward the air. "We were going up this ridge, and this crazy driver rammed his truck into my dad's car…we flew off the ridge. I was in a coma for three months. When I woke up, I couldn't see…the most hardened thing to live with was that my dad, mom, and brother died instantly."

I felt teardrops on my arm. My eyes began to water up. The blood drained from my body, and my heart ached for her. She suffered a great deal of loss. I wrapped my arms around her. She buried her face in my arms. Sobbing.

"Then I asked myself what I did to deserve *this?!* What couldn't I die with them?!" She shook her head back and forth, "And I asked God what did *I* do to deserve this punishment?!"

I felt tears flow down my cheek. She was frantically sobbing, releasing all that was built in her.

"I should have been with them?! I should have been with them?!" She kept repeating that to herself.

I gently rubbed her shoulders.

"It's okay." As my hand went up and down her arm. I wiped the tears from my eyes. "God needed you here to heal the world *that's why you're here;* we need an extra you to make this world better."

I kissed her head. I picked up my magazine and began reading my article to her:

Why Stop at Ground Level

By Seth Calloway

Why do we stop at our lowest potential instead of reaching for our fullest potential?

I spoke with CEO Jonathan Webb, who said that people only seek opportunities that are comfortable for them instead of going for higher levels…

CHAPTER 5

I *love* her. I love her from the kinky coils of her hair, down to the crevice of her toe. From the inner beauty of her soul to the outer beauty of a portrait. Every imperfection is covered with colors that I don't see…because I see only *her*. I'm *infatuated* with how she sees the world through her paintings. Sometimes when she paints, instead of me painting with her, I sit by and watch her. Then I take out my journal and write. I write at home. I write at work.

Day and days on, we spend a lot of time together. I went with her family to Six Flags. I've been a few times, and Chelsea has only been once when she had her sight. So, I thought it would be nice to spend some time together with her family. Kyla took my hand and escorted us to every ride. "Let's go this way! Come *on* Uncle Seth, we have to get in line."

I laughed and went with her. I like the name Uncle Seth. I could see it. I squeezed Chelsea's hand. "We're about to enter the Batman ride, I pressed on. Your legs will be hanging down."

"I think I'm going to sit down, and you have your fun with that."

"Come on, it's a fun ride."

Joseph chimed in. "Yes, we are going into a dark cave. Ooo!" Making ghost sounds at us.

She shook her head.

"Come on, I will hold your hand." I grab her arm and lock it in mine. We head to the roller coaster. When we made it to the line, I strapped her into the seat. I got myself strapped, and we took off. I held her hand for a moment until she released me. I looked at her, and there she was, screaming and laughing with her hands lifted in the air. After the ride, I help her out of the seat.

"I want to ride it again. It was fun!" she said excitedly.

"All right, let's go!"

I guided her arm from the exit and returned back to the entrance. I have noticed one thing about her that's changed since we've been spending a lot of time together. Her grip around my arm has softened a bit. She used to hold on tight as if every step was super critical. But now, she let me lead her.

After the second go of the Batman, we got a bit thirsty. I found the next food stand to get some bottles of water and a bit of rest.

Joseph, Tamara, and Kyla met us at the stand.

"Which ride are we heading to next?" Joseph asked. "Or do you want to find a place to eat? I'm getting kind of hungry."

"I want to get on the carousel!" Kyla pleaded. "We passed by it, and you promised we would get to ride it, Daddy."

"Ok, Niña, we are heading to the carousel."

"Yay! Come on Uncle Seth!"

She pulled my hand to follow her to the carousel. Tamara helped Chelsea along the way. Kyla and I were so far in pace that we were almost about to leave the rest of the group. When I turned to see their location, I saw Chelsea whisper something in Tamara's ears and they giggled. I'm so glad she has them, I thought. She went through a whole ordeal, and she had family to stick with her.

All families need to stick together.

"It's a line!" Kyla stomped her foot and crossed her arms across her chest.

"It will go fast" I assured her. "It's not that many people at the park today."

The rest of the group met us in the line. I went back to join Chelsea. I wrapped my arms around her.

"Hey, there," I whispered.

"Hey, you." she wrapped her arms around my waist. I kissed her forehead.

"Have you gotten on a horse before?"

She laughed.

"Yes, I've been on plenty of carousels. Back home, we had an amusement park there called Lake Winnipesauke-nothing Six

Flags, but it was still fun."

"When was the last time you went back home?"

"Not since the accident."

"Why not? Do you still have family out there?"

"Yes, I do. I miss home. Sometimes they come here to see me, but I haven't gone there yet."

"Come on, you guys!" yelled Kyla.

We walk onto the carousel.

After the carousel, we went to a burger joint and got ourselves a meal. I got a cheeseburger with the works and a fry basket. Chelsea got a chicken sandwich and a fry basket. Joseph and his crew ordered burgers and fries as well. After we ate, we rode more rides. After the rides, we walked around eating cotton candy, funnel cakes, and Dipping Dots. We stayed at Six Flags till it was time to close. They were going to have a fireworks show afterward to celebrate the theme park's anniversary. Joseph took Kyla and Chelsea to the fireworks. Tamara and I walked to the cars. I wanted a moment to privately talk to Tamara.

"Hey Seth," she said placing the prizes they won in the car.

"Did you enjoy yourself?"

"Oh yeah, most definitely! Hey, I'm a daredevil-this is what I do."

She laughed. "I used to be and *then* I got older. Chelsea seems to be having a blast. I think she's quite fond of you."

"Yeah, I am fond of her too."

"Now don't you go and break her heart now. Cause I will get *beast mode* on you quickly. That's my little sis, her heart is more fragile."

"I won't." I paused a moment, "Can I ask something? Why doesn't she ever go back to her hometown?"

"Well, we've tried a few times before, but she never seemed to want to go. I think it's painful for her, the memories of family being there. I try to do things at her own pace because I don't want to pressure or suffocate her, causing her to withdraw or isolate herself. Because it *has* happened a few times before, and it's not an easy thing to see that or console her." She sighed deeply and glanced towards the direction of the show. "I can only imagine what she may be feeling. That's why I've been right beside her ever since."

I saw the pain in her eyes on how she spoke about Chelsea. Her eyes began to water. "Do you think she'll ever show her paintings?"

"No... but I think you'll show them."

"She is very talented. She shouldn't try to hide it." I said. "If *anyone*, I must need your support on this matter.

"No, she shouldn't… but let that be her decision, not yours."

She finished putting all their things in the car. "You're a good guy Seth."

She smiled at me.

BAM! BAM! POP

The fireworks show started and we turned to watch. I saw the child in her that day. She *felt* like a child all over again. We need to have child-like moments to remind us of fun, innocence, and joy.

The next day we went to the zoo. I invited Cynthia and her kids to come with us. It was too hot in the day for it to be October. There was a bit of a cool draft when the wind would blow. We went around looking at the animals. Chelsea absorbs all the many different sounds of the animals and their smells. I told Chelsea she needed to really appreciate my scent because these animal scents were tainted. She laughed and playfully hit me on the arm.

"I love your scent," she whispered.

I wrap my arm around her. I notice my sister watching from a distance. I made a face, and she laughed.

"I think we should go feed the animals. You want to do that?" I asked.

"Of course!"

We went to the animal encounter section of the zoo. The first encounter that was showcased was a baby elephant. The zookeeper was talking to the group all about the elephant, their meals, their ways, and how they adjust at the zoo. The elephant was protected by a fence. The associate gave us each a plant to feed to the elephant. The elephant's name was Cairo. He was very friendly and hungry because he stayed in the same spot wanting to be fed. His trunk was hanging from one of the holes in the fence.

"Cairo is a bit frisky with the food." I reached to touch his snout.

"Here, I'm going to let you feed him." I gently grab her hand. "I want you to feel the plant in your hand." I gently place her free hand on the food. "There you go; he's going to quickly snatch it." I used both my hands to lean her toward the fence.

With a quick sweep, Cairo snatched the plant and put it in his mouth.

"Aw," she breathed.

Cairo placed his trunk back in the same hole to get some more food.

"Here he goes again; I'm going to let you feel his trunk. Open your hands." I said.

I did guide her hands to the fence. She slowly leaned forward with her hand outstretched. Cairo slowly outstretched his trunk to touch her hand. And they touched. Chelsea gently rubbed his trunk and Cairo just stayed there.

"It feels rubbery" she laughed.

We continued to make our way through the zoo. We entered the monkey kingdom where there were different breeds of monkeys. It was a zoo trainer in the area, a monkey hung over his shoulder. The kids got excited.

"Mom, can we go see the monkey?" they said in unison.

"Yes, go ahead, that's what we're here for."

"I would like to go with them" Chelsea volunteered. "I just need someone to take me."

Mariah went and took Chelsea's hand. "I will take you. The man has a real monkey on his shoulder!"

"Maybe he will let us pet him."

Mariah led Chelsea in the monkey kingdom. I yelled, "Don't leave Chelsea by herself."

"We won't!" they yelled in response.

My sister and I walked to a nearby bench and sat down. We were quiet at first; I'm sure she knew as well as I the topic at hand that needed to be addressed- Dad. The last conversation I had with my siblings about my dad was us needing to just throw him in the car unwillingly and force him to see the doctor. But one visit wouldn't guarantee the next or the next after. Still, we need to see what needs to be done because Dad was being stubborn about the whole thing. Even though I'm the baby of the family, it would definitely sound a whole lot better coming from my sister. Sometimes women have a way of getting things done when a man can't.

"I think Dad's sick and he's not saying anything about it." I started.

"I know, we went over there to see him the other day. He was passed out on the couch, and Luke ran into the kitchen and said Grandpa has a nosebleed. When I ran in there, he was quickly trying to wipe his nose. I told him I was taking him to the emergency room, but he pitched a fit. I don't know what else to do. He's not listening to me. Milton and I were thinking maybe hiring a nurse who can sit in with him, but that would be expensive."

"Yeah, and he wouldn't agree to it. He would run the nurse out or *find* ways to."

"Well, you, Zach, and I need to figure this out and soon. I don't want to think about losing Daddy. We lost Mom and I just don't want to go through that."

"I know, everything will be all right; it's up to Dad if he wants the help. We can do all we can, but it takes the individual to want to."

"Well, you know Dad has a hard head like *you* do!?"

"What?! *I* have a hard head?" I pointed to myself, "If you don't get your Velociraptor toes on somewhere! You can cut through skin with your toes!"

We burst out laughing.

After the zoo, I took Chelsea to the botanical gardens. Cynthia and the kids left because she had to pick up her husband and get dinner started. I saw flowers in a lot of the portraits that Chelsea draws, so what better place to take her for the experience? She was teaching me the names of the flowers she knew and their color. She said that she learned about flowers and gardening at the blind school that she attended. Her teacher, Mrs. Hawkins, made sure the students learned the right tools and seeds in which to plant, how much water and sun each plant needs, and the season in which to plant them.

"One day when I have a house, I would love to have a garden," Chelsea said.

"What's your favorite flower?" I asked.

"A poinsettia."

We went to my dad's house for dinner and a game. Zachary stopped by because he heard I was coming with Chelsea. Dad still hasn't gone to see a doctor yet. I'm just hoping that whatever is going on doesn't take a turn for the worse… if it hasn't already. I was taken by how Dad was having fun with Chelsea even though she was rooting for the opposite team. She said it's fun that way. "My dad was always for the underdogs. You have to give them a chance he would say." When my dad's team made a fumble, Chelsea cheered to it.

"Yay!"

My dad would say, "Hey *now*-!"

Then they'd laugh together. I sat back and enjoyed the wings.

***

It was mid-November, and the air was beginning to be chilly. I had something thought up today that I knew Chelsea would enjoy. Christmas activities have already started. I decided to take Chelsea on a Christmas Carriage ride in the park and get tickets to the Nutcracker. I told Tamara in advance what I planned on doing, so she could get her outfit ready for the day. I wanted us to coordinate our outfits together, a red sweater and black pants. Chelsea was ready when I picked her up.

Once we made it to the park, I helped her out of the car.

"I got a surprise for you today," I said to her.

"What is it?"

"Well, we're at the park, and we're about to climb into a sleigh. We're going on a Christmas sleigh ride in the park."

I led her to the sleigh.

"Aw, moments like these I wish I could see."

"You *can* see it. The sleigh is red with garland and holly decorated on it. There's a white horse that will be pulling the sleigh. Santa and Mrs. Claus will be holding the reins."

When we approach Santa and Mrs. Claus, they hand us bells, hot chocolate, and a bag of assorted candy.

"Ah, y'all look so cute together," said Mrs. Claus.

I helped her into the sleigh, and we rode around the park. It was a bit breezy; luckily, they suggested that I bring a blanket just in case. I covered our legs with the blanket. We were jingling our bells and singing Christmas carols- *Jingle Bells, Winter Wonderland, God Rest Ye Merry Gentlemen, Hark the Herald*, and more.

The man who was dressed up as Santa turned his head to us and said, "We're about to enter Santa's Workshop."

Chelsea squealed out in excitement. "Yay!" She squeezed my arm. "What is it like?!"

"It's beautiful Chel!" I told her what I saw.

The scenery was beautiful, and how the lights were displayed. The display of colors, plus the beaming of lights, was fantastic. It had elves mechanically fixing on toys, and you could hear the sound of a conveyor belt moving the toys along. They were singing *Santa Claus is coming to town*.

"You must *really* love elves," I said.

"Yes, I do. You know, people always say how much Christmas can be commercial. But Christmas is *really* all about how you make it. You have Santa and his elves, the helpers. But we have God and his angels-*our* helpers. And when you look at it, we're his helpers too.

Santa Claus turned around and said, "Wow, I never thought it that way. I'm going to have to start saying that."

Mrs. Claus smiled and gave us a wink. The irony in her statement made you stop and think-

Wow! That's so true! If only the world thought this way.

There was one part of the ride where we stopped, and I took her out to bring her into this archway that was decorated in mistletoes. I pressed my lips to hers and we kissed. We kissed at the Nutcracker, too. I don't remember much about the show. I just watched her as her face gleamed with excitement.

***

I was excited. I was going to meet Seth's friends and we're going to have a game night. I've always loved playing games. I just never played while I was with someone. I wonder if we were going to play couples games or team games. We were going over JP's house for the gathering. I couldn't wait to meet JP; I know Seth talks about him a lot. I wanted to make sure I looked nice, so I asked Tamara if she could find something cute and comfortable. I made my way downstairs for Seth to pick me up. Of course, he was always on time.

In the car, I was starting to get a bit nervous. I wonder what they'll think about me. Do they think that I will be a right fit for Seth?

"Are you okay?" he asked me.

He must've been watching as he was driving.

"Yes, I'm good."

"You will like them. They're really cool people."

"How many will there be?"

"I don't know, maybe around six to eight people, depending on who's all coming. I'm excited. I love playing games."

"Yes, I like games too."

The car was beginning to slow down, and it turned into a driveway. So, I know that we've reached our destination. He opened the car and got out. *Here* we go, I thought to myself. Friends can sometimes be hard to please. I didn't want them to feel uncomfortable since I was blind. I held on to his arm and he guided me to the house.

He whispered, "There are six steps in front of you."

We start the climb. When we made it to the third step, I heard a door burst open. "Hey man, y'all finally made it. Everyone is *here* you know."

I felt Seth give him a hug. I was curious about that statement because it sounded as if he was warning him someone was there.

"You must be Chelsea!"

I reached out my hand and he took it and shook it rather hard.

"I'm JP as you can tell. I'm sure your man here has told you a lot of things about me. You're cute-you don't look blind!" "Dude!" Seth said.

"What?!" JP asked.

"It's okay; I'd rather for you to be comfortable. But I get that a lot." I said laughing. I heard another voice coming.

"Babe, let her breathe," a voice said.

"She's breathing!" JP responded.

"Don't mind my husband, my name is Lizzy."

"Chelsea." I replied.

She shook my hand and grabbed my arm to guide me into the house. She guided me into a room, which I assumed was probably the living room.

"Everyone this is Seth's lady friend; her name is Chelsea."

All at once I heard footsteps coming my way. One by one, they would come to shake my hand "I'm Mia"

"Tony"

"Alexander but you can call me Alex."

"I'm Chloe."

"Kristy."

Kristy didn't shake my hand. Her tone was dismissive. As if she wanted to brush me off. I felt Seth's gentle hand guide me to the seat. I sat down on a sofa right beside Seth. There was someone next to me. By her smell, it was Chloe. I picked up on each person's scent. "So what game are we playing?" asked Alex.

"We can play Pictionary," Lizzy suggested.

"I don't think that's good came for you know who," said Kristy

The obvious she was implying me since I'm blind, I wouldn't be able to play. "Well, we can ask Chelsea if she would like to play." Lizzy clapped back.

I can tell Lizzy feels the same way as I do about Kristy. "I don't mind playing" I chimed.

"We will do it together when it's our turn." Seth included.

"Whatever," Kristy retorts.

If I could see, I'm sure Kristy was shooting daggers at me. Her tone is very off-putting. There must have been something going on with her and Seth. I'm not going to let her spoil my fun. Everyone seemed to be really cool and inviting. We played Pictionary. Seth and I worked together on both games. For Pictionary, when it was our turn, we would walk up there together. He would whisper the name in my ear. If I knew how to draw it, I would, and if not, he would. At one point, I did hear Kristy say to someone "I didn't know that they were able to draw."

I was about to turn around and stick it to her, but I let it go. Some people can be ignorant of what they don't know. Everyone else made me feel comfortable. Seth would always squeeze my arm or whisper something funny in my ear. Then to top that off, across the way I would hear her say "Oh Seth this..." or "Oh Seth that..." She was really bugging me.

On the car ride home, we were quiet for the most part. I did have a good time. Everyone wanted me to come back-*well* of course not *everyone*, but I did say I would do it again. Seth reached over to pull my hand to his mouth to kiss it.

"I had a good time."

"Did you?" he asked. "How did you like everyone?"

"I did have fun. Everyone was nice. I wasn't for sure about Kristy though."

"I'm sorry. Kristy and I dated some time ago-it was very short, and nothing came from it."

"Oh."

I didn't think he would volunteer that information. I thought I was going to have to probe and ask questions. But it was short.. Just like their relationship was short. But the book may have closed on his end, not hers. Obviously, there were some feelings she still had with him. I just hope that it stays short-lived.

"How does she look?"

"*What?!*"

"I want to know how she looks, Seth."

"She's short, light-skinned, medium hair. I don't know really how else much to describe her."

"Is she pretty?"

Pause.

"Yes, she is. But I'm not interested in her. Trust me." We pulled up to my driveway.

"It looks like your cousins aren't home. Do you have a key?" "Yes, they are at a cabin this weekend."

He walked me to the door, and I used the spare key to open it. I quickly walked to the kitchen to turn off the security alarm.

"Do you want to come in?"

"Yes, I want to make sure everything is okay before I leave."

We walked in the house. Seth left me in the living room while he went to check to make sure every door and window was locked.

"I checked everything; everything looks good. I'm glad they have a security alarm in the house."

I reached my arm out to follow where his voice was so that I could touch him.

"I want to show you something."

I grabbed his hand and led him up the stairs. I opened the door to my room and let him walk in. "Wow! You did all *this?!*" he exclaimed.

I nodded. "Some of my pictures are also displayed in Mr. Chaplin's studio."

In my room, was a collage full of pictures on the wall of the things that I've painted. I hear him walking from the picture and his hand rubbing against the portrait. Then he stopped.

"That's a picture of my dad, mom, and brother," I said.

"It's amazing, Chelsea! So detailed…. you have a beautiful family."

I walked to my dresser to pull out a gift I wanted to give him. "I got something for you." We sat on the bed, and he opened his gift.

"A digital camera! This is really nice!"

"Yeah, just for whenever you go on your journey. I want you to take lots of pictures. That way, you have something to write about in your magazine column."

I felt his arms wrap around me. "Thank you." "I figured you need one." There was a long pause.

"Stop looking at me," I said and looked the other way.

"How do you know I *was* looking at you?"

"I can feel you looking."

"Well, I think you're pretty." I felt his hand touch my arm. "I like looking at you."

"I don't!" I rubbed my hand up and down my arm, "I don't…feel…pretty." My eyes started tearing up.

It's easy for him to say that. Or for someone to say that to someone…but my feelings were different. How can he love me when there are so many beautiful women in the world? Women, who *have* their sight, I thought to myself.

I felt his hand caress my face. He brought his face close to mine, and I felt the warmth of his breath on my skin. I closed my eyes as he planted a kiss one by one across my face. Then he cupped my face in his hand.

"Open your eyes…I want you to *see* me." And I opened them.

His lips found me, and I lost myself within him. I *tasted* every part of him as his tongue made gentle strokes into mine. As I planted kisses onto his skin, I tasted the smooth, silk skin of his body. He took off his shirt and lowered my head onto the bed. My hands *touched* his chest, and I felt the hardness of his body. I felt the softness of the rapid beat of his heart and slid my hands to his back. The *smell* of his body was *his* scent but only sweeter…sweeter… and sweeter the more we kissed. I could *hear* the soft moans from our mouths and our bodies intertwine together. He stayed with me the rest of the night. His warmth was wrapped around me as he held me close to him.

"I love you," he whispered in my ear.

I loved him, but I couldn't say it. I wasn't ready to say it.

I have to love me before I can love anyone else. When I love myself, then I can see that I *am* beautiful. Chelsea, you… *are*… beautiful. And I have to answer back, yes, I am. I *know* that I am!

If only I could see a mirror.

***

Kristy made it home. She stays in luxurious condo located north on Peachtree. She took off her shoes and threw them on the floor. Then she walked to her wine bar to get her favorite Chardonnay and popped the cork right out. She indulged in almost half the wine bottle before flopping on her couch. She picks up her phone and runs through her camera photos. She stops at the picture of her and Seth. I thought we were sooooo happy together. What makes her so much better than me? I look so much better than she does.

"Seth, you can't get rid of me that fast baby." She drank some more from her bottle.

"I'm going to make you mine, Seth. You're not going to say *no* to me this time." She smirked at the picture.

"You want be able to keep him."

CHAPTER 6

Sleep was my enemy. I tossed and turned; I even stared at the blank wall. I was up all night finishing up the presentation that I was going to present to Mrs. Decker. I am going to bring the portrait that Chelsea said I could keep, and I'm presenting the article behind this masterpiece, "A blind student whose art is untouchable." I'm sure that after she sees what I have, she will be open to any ideas that I come up with. I'm sure the readers will be pouring out responses from this article. Once they see her paintings, it will open up new doors for Chelsea. We can launch this magazine in a new direction, make it expand more globally, I would say. I will have the freedom to put real, raw materials that people will love. This could be the turning point in my career that I have been waiting for... But to who's expense? Mine? Chelsea's? I'm sure she won't be *that* mad at me. I just have to make her understand that this story needs to be told to inspire other people to reach for their potential, use their gifts, and not waste them.

Man, I hope she understands, I thought to myself as I made my way to turn on the showerhead. A fifteen-minute shower turned into forty-five minutes. I just let the water spray beat on my head.

Man, why do I feel so guilty?

I made my way into the office. I decided I would go to Mrs. Decker's office first thing in the morning when I knew she would definitely be in her office. If I miss the morning, I could forget about the rest of the day because she will be unavailable. That's when she only sees *you* instead of you seeing *her.* I told JP all that

I was about to do, and he thinks it's a good idea. But he also said I should run it by Chelsea first, which I'm not going to do, not yet, anyway. If I don't do it now, then I will never do it. It will be a missed opportunity for me. I know Chelsea wouldn't like it, but it's for her best interest. I'm here, so I'm going for it. I went inside the elevator and pushed the button on the 8th floor. The only office on the 8th floor was Mrs. Decker's office. The higher-ups were the floors extended above the 8th. The 8th floor was only Mrs. Decker's office, a kitchen, a conference room, a showroom, and a secretary desk that's right off the elevator.

"Hello, how may I help you?" the secretary asked.

"I just need to speak to Mrs. Decker for a brief moment," I replied.

"Unfortunately, Mrs. Decker isn't seeing anyone today. I can schedule a meeting with her next month or the month after."

"Her door is wide open. I need to speak to her now."

Mrs. Decker raised her head from her desk and looked at me.

"It's ok, Anna, I will see him," she shouted.

I walked into her office and closed the door.

"Seth, what's so urgent that you need to see?" She didn't even look up from flipping through a magazine. "Well, this better be good. I have palettes here in the next thirty minutes."

"It is good."

I turned the portrait to her so she could see it.

"Nice," she said dryly. "Is this all?"

"No, it isn't!"

I put down my folder and flipped through the pages of each.

She looked at one nodding her head.

"These paintings are all done by a *blind* student! She sits in an art studio and paints whatever comes to her mind."

"Wow!" The pictures caused a spark in her eyes. She was studying each portrait as she flipped through the portfolio. "This is very impressive-I wouldn't mind having some hung up in my house *or* this office."

"She wasn't born blind either. She lost her sight by some freak incident."

"What incident?"

"I don't know." I lied.

"Well, found out!" She demanded. "I want this on the cover of the next issue."

"Ok, will do!"

"Seth, very good work! I look forward to reading the article in your column."

"*My...column?*" I asked.

"That's what I said. Now, you have work to do."

"Oh y-yes," I stammered with excitement.

I left her office feeling vindicated in my work. I feel really good about this. I can write this article in *my* column. I don't even know what I should title *my* column. Of course, it has to have something that represents Chelsea. This is all because of her after all. I just have to find the nerve to tell her what I have done and what I'm about to do. Maybe it won't be as bad as how I would think it would be. Oh, Chelsea, I just want to make you happy.

***

"Wake up, Chelsea!" I was moving her shoulders to wake her up from bed.

"Mm," she said and turned her head.

"Wake up and get dress."

"Mm, what time is it? And how did you get in my room?"

"It's nine o'clock in the morning, and your cousin invited me in."

"I don't get up until ten, come back and wake me up then." She flipped the covers over her head.

I flipped her covers back.

"Come on, baby, I want to take you somewhere, and it's a drive."

"Where?" she grumbled.

"It's a surprise. Now wake up and get dressed."

"Okay, I can't get dress until you *leave*!"

I laughed. "I am leaving now." I walked out of her room and went back downstairs. Tamara was already in the kitchen fixing up some breakfast. Kyla was up and already on the couch watching cartoons.

"Before y'all go, please sit down and put something in your stomachs," Tamara said. "I made plenty of food."

"Ok, we can spare an hour for sustenance."

I was going to enjoy the meal indeed. Tamara whipped up some bacon, sausage links with crispy edges, toast, grits, and some homemade biscuits and gravy. Joseph came down and scrambled the eggs. He threw in some peppers, onions, spices, and cheese. It was the bomb! The food was so good that I almost forgot why I came over in the first place. Chelsea was dressed and came downstairs to eat as well.

After breakfast, we hit the highway. I told her to bring her stick just in case since it would be new territory for me. I made sure the gas was full, and the spare tire was in the trunk as well as some jumper cables. I have a new car, but you still need to have a safety kit as a backup. Dad always made sure to check those off the list before a travel. We were off.

"I bought plenty of snacks for us. There's chips, crackers, and sweets in the back seat if you get hungry. Plus, there's some water bottles in case you get thirsty."

"Okay, you sure had this way planned out for me."

"Yes, I did."

"And we're going where again?"

"Ha! It's still a surprise."

I reached out and turned the radio on. The radio station was playing Rihanna's *We Found Love*. Chelsea starts belting out the lyrics to the song. That was my first time hearing her sing and she has a pretty nice voice.

"So, you can sing, but you *said* you can't dance. But you *can* dance. You're confusing me now."

"I never told you I *couldn't* sing. Sometimes, a lady likes to be mysterious."

"Oh, I *see* that!"

We laughed and listened to music all the way to Chattanooga.

The drive took just about two hours when we finally made it to Chattanooga. I took the next exit off the ramp that said North Moore Road because I needed to go straight to the gas station to get some gas. I was a quart near empty and this was the first stop of the drive here. I made it to the gas station and pumped the gas.

After I was done, I got back in the car.

"We made it!"

"Yes, Chattanooga isn't that far from Atlanta," she said.

"How did you know we were in Chattanooga?"

"Because the radio station switched to Power94, and that's the station I listened to when I was a little girl. Plus, it wasn't a long drive, and this was the only place that I talked to you about."

"You're a very smart person."

"Yes, but Seth, I wish you would have asked me."

"I know, but you wouldn't have agreed. Do you want us to head back?"

"No, you're fine."

"Where do you want to head to first?"

"I don't know. Where would you like to go?"

"I want to see where you lived."

"1204 North Parkdale Avenue."

"Wow you still remember your old address?"

"I won't ever forget it."

I put the coordinates in my Google map. It was approximately ten minutes from the gas station.

"We're right down the street from it?"

"Then we must be in the area of Brainerd," she said familiarly.

"I guess so."

I started the car, and we headed to the location. On the way there, Chelsea was quiet. I hoped I made the right decision in bringing her here. I thought she needed this closure to move on—to find peace within herself. I wanted to show her that she doesn't have to be alone. I continued driving until it said I had reached my destination. I pulled into the driveway of a single-level home. It had a creamy peach tint to it with black shudders. There was a wide porch in the front, with a bench and two chairs placed on it. I assumed there wasn't a deck on the back because the grill was placed in the front. I got out of the car.

"Are we here?" she asked.

"I think so," I replied. "Does it have a peach color tint with black shudders?"

"Is there a birdbath in front of the home?"

"Yes."

"Then this my home," she replied.

"Are you okay?" She nodded.

"Ok, you stay here. Let me see if someone's home."

I got out of the car and walked up to the porch. I saw a doorbell and rang it.

No answer.

I rang it again.

I heard footsteps inside, and then a lady came to the door. She appeared to be maybe in her early to mid-sixties. Her hair was pinned into a scarf. And when she opened her door, I smelled a hint of cinnamon and nutmeg. There was a security door right between.

"Yes, how may I help you?"

"Yes, my name is Seth Callaway. My girlfriend, Chelsea Davis, used to live her years with her parents. Unfortunately, her parents passed away. We were wondering if we could just walk around the property. It would mean a lot to her."

The lady was put off for a moment taking it all in. I continued.

"My girlfriend who lived here is blind now."

"I think I remember that being told to me when I first purchased the home. My name is Loretta. Of course, y'all can."

I nodded. I walk off the steps to help Chelsea out of the car. She took her pole and felt around the grass.

"Point me in the direction of the birdbath."

I turned her body in that direction, and she used her stick to follow her the rest of the way. When she made it to the bed bath, she used her hands to fall around the bath. She lifted her hands in the air to feel for the bird feeder. She laughed.

"It's still here."

My heart broke for her. I almost got choked up watching her embrace the nostalgia moment of her home-the feel, the sound, and the smell. I placed my arm around her.

"I'm so overwhelmed with emotion." She turned her head over to her right. "There's a tree over there, it's a dogwood. Every spring it will blossom with its white, beautiful flowers. It was my mom's favorite tree."

Tears streamed down her face. I rubbed her arms.

"Seth, I want you to take me to their cemetery."

"I will."

I led her back into the car. When I went inside my car, I looked up to see Mrs. Loretta standing in the doorway. I waved at her and she waved back. I got back in the car. I asked her what the name of the cemetery was and put the location in my phone's GPS. We headed in the direction of – Lakewood-. She was quiet again on the way there. I turned off the radio because I didn't know if it was a distraction. She needs her moment. As soon as we got there, I had to call to speak to someone so she could give me the location of their tombstones. It was a huge cemetery, very beautiful. It took a moment to find their exact location, but I was able to get us there.

I took her out of the car, and we began to walk. She stopped midway.

She tightened her grip on my arm.

"I don't think I can do this." She was shaking her head, and tears began to fall.

"Yes, you can, I will be right here with you."

"I only had been here once. And when we were here, I stayed in the car because I just couldn't bring myself to see them. I don't think I can do it."

"Yes, you can." I held her close to me, "You have to make *peace* within *yourself* to heal from this Chelsea. It wasn't your fault in anything okay? In this life, we all have to suffer death, hardships, sickness, and struggles...and when they come, it is God's way of love to show us that he will be there with us *every* step of the way. We all go through things, no one is alone. No one is singled out, even when we think that we are. That's why when one hurts, we all hurt." Tears streamed from my eyes.

She nodded and slowly started walking with me. I stopped once we made it to the tombstones. There were two big tombstones for both her mom and dad. There was a smaller tombstone placed in front for her brother. She reached her hand out until she felt the tombstones. Then she dropped to her knees and started crying. I walked back a few feet so that she could be alone with them. We were there for a while. I didn't care if it took a couple of days; I wanted to be there for her. When she was done, she called my name to come over. I walked over and helped her to the car. When we left the cemetery and got out onto the main road, she whispered, "Thank you".

The day was winding down into the early evening; I was riding around the town for a moment.

"Are you hungry? I can pull up somewhere and give us a bite to eat."

"Yeah, I'm hungry too."

I pulled into a grilled steakhouse restaurant. It was surrounded by other eatery places, but this spoke to me because I wanted some meat. I was that much hungry. I pulled into the parking and help Chelsea from the car. The aroma of the place made my stomach growl even more.

"The food smells good," she said as we approached the door. "Have you had eaten before?"

"No, not that I can remember."

"Do you like steak?

"Yes- I don't eat it as often, but I may order one today." Inside people were standing around.

"Well, it looks like we are going to have to wait. Do you want to wait or go someplace else?" I asked her.

"No, we can wait. I'm sure if we go to some other place, it will be the same way."

"Ok, well, let me find us a seat while we wait."

I looked around, but every spot was full. Then a white gentle-man, who looked like he was in his mid-thirties, approached us.

"If she needs to sit down, she can have my seat." The gentleman offered.

"Aw, thanks, man!" I said to him.

I placed her on the seat.

"I'll be right back; I'm going to put our names on the list."

I turned around and left to approach the hostess to tell her there were going to be two needing a table. She added our names on the list and said that it was be thirty-minute wait time. I turned around to return to Chelsea who was sitting by the door. As I turned, there was an older man, who couldn't have been much older than sixty, who walked in and tripped on Chelsea's cane, which was slightly turned out. He stumbled onto the floor. His wife ran up.

"Are you ok?"

Embarrassed, he leaped up and started yelling at Chelsea.

"You need to get that damn thing out of the way!" He shouted at her.

I rushed over there to him.

"Whoa, whoa, whoa!" I put my hand up. "You don't need to talk to her that way, seriously man!"

"*Who are you?!*"

"*You don't need to worry about who I am! I don't know you and you don't know me!*" My anger was there with him. I look him straight in the eye without a flinch. He kept on going.

"Well, she needs to get *that* off the floor".

He was beginning to back off as his wife quickly approached to grab his arm. "Come on, dear."

"*You* don't need to address her! She keeps her cane wherever she needs to keep it. She's blind! *You* need to watch where you stepping! That's what you need to do!!!"

I completely lost myself. I was standing until he walked to the side of the room with his fist clenched up. I was turned all the way up. Like *really?!* You want to go to that level just because you tripped! I've tripped a million times in my life, but I've never gotten to a point where I yelled at someone. Sometimes I tripped and laughed at my own damn self. I turned around and the gentleman, who offered to give us his seat, went over to pick up Chelsea's cane and gave it to her. He shook his head. "What is this world coming to when you attack those who can't defend themselves?" Exactly?! Especially when it comes to women and children!

What is this world coming to?

If I wasn't here to defend her, no telling what he may have said extra or done. All he had to do was stop and look. Stop and look that's it! I stood there and thought, how impactful situations will turn out for the better if we just stop for a second... listen for a moment...respond not as often.

The waiting area was quiet because of the commotion. I was sitting next to Chelsea, waiting for our names to be called. I was so hungry before but now it's as if I don't want to eat anything.

Chelsea touched my arm and then slowly wrapped her arms in mine. She laid her head on my arm.

"Are you okay?" she asked.

"Yes, just ready to eat," I said gently.

"Liar. Your muscles are tense."

I laughed and wrapped my arm around her. "I'm okay. How are you doing?"

"I'm good. I was thinking the next time we come back here. I'll have to introduce you to my family."

"I'm all game."

After dinner, we hit the highway to head back home. I turned the radio back on and we listened to it more instead of singing. Chattanooga seems like a nice town to visit, and it's right down the road to break away from the big city. I'm happy Chelsea is in a comfortable space with her past. This is her home *with* beautiful, shared memories of her and her family; she shouldn't have to keep that in the dark.

CHAPTER 7

I was asleep when the phone rang.

It was Seth.

"Hey, I'm coming to get you; they had to rush my dad to the hospital."

"Ok, I'll get up." I said quickly.

I got up and hurried to get dressed. It was only just a couple of days ago; we went and picked Mr. Callaway up to take him to the Cheesecake Factory. Everything seemed fine to me. I know he was coughing just a bit, but it was nothing abnormal from the previous occurrences.

What seemed like minutes was only seconds when Seth picked me up to go to the emergency room. I just threw on some loose clothes from the closet and brushed my hair into a ponytail.

"What happened?" I didn't fully have my seatbelt on when Seth zoomed from the driveway. "Have you spoken to him yet?"

"My brother called me just a moment ago because Dad wasn't answering his phone. When he went over to check, my dad was lying unconscious on the ground. He quickly called 911."

"Oh my!"

I reached over to rub his leg. I didn't think about what could be going on with Mr. Callaway. I just hope he's fine. The last time I was in the hospital, I was in a coma for three months. And from then on, I still had to go back for physical therapy, therapy itself, and treatments. I like to avoid hospitals as much as I can. I'm glad I can be here for Seth. I didn't want him to go through any of this on his own. Whatever *this* may be. Seth got on his phone, talking to his sister that we had arrived.

Once we entered the hospital, Cynthia met us and took us up to Mr. Callaway's room. When we got into the room, Seth directed me to the nearest chair. I heard the sound of a monitor beeping. I didn't feel Seth near me; I could hear him close to the monitor.

"Have the doctors said what's wrong with him?"

"No, they don't know as of right now; they are still running tests," Zach said.

"He's still unconscious. He was dehydrated too, so there's an extra tube that they have in him to get his fluids going." Cynthia sat in the seat beside me. It's cold in here, are you cold?" she asked me.

"No." I just shook my head.

I was a bit hungry though. I wasn't going to say anything at the moment. It was quite a moment. Eventually, I heard Zach say that he was going to cut on the TV. He was going from channel to channel because I could hear a different sound every few seconds. I highly doubt anybody was even watching the TV. Seth was pacing here and there for a moment, the sound of his shoe echoing in the room, or at least my ear. I think he eventually found someplace to sit down because it abruptly stopped. I wished I could do something for them, but I didn't know what else more that I could do except to sit here. I silently said a prayer to God that Mr.

Calloway would be ok.

It was nearly five hours, and we haven't heard anything as of yet. Nurses would come in to check his IV and do their regular routine. Seth would ask if they heard anything, and the response always was the same: "The doctor hasn't informed them of anything." In the meantime, Seth went to the cafeteria to get us some sandwiches and chips. It didn't taste like much, but I gulped it down anyway. I needed to get something on my stomach. Seth was sitting next to me. I don't think he ate much of anything. He was just so quiet. I've never seen him like this before. Here and there, he will give my arm a squeeze, but never a sound. Thanksgiving was only a couple of days from now, but for the Calloway family, it's just another day right now. *Please let us have another football game together,* I thought to myself. We have so much fun watching football together.

Sitting with him reminded me of just sitting there with my dad as he is tuned into the game.

Knock. Knock.

The door opened.

I heard the noise of shoes clicking on the floor.

"Hello, I'm Dr. Adams, I'm the emergency doctor here in the emergency room. There's a bit of bad news regarding your dad. I take it you're his children?"

"Yes, I'm his daughter and these are my brothers."

"There are two things I wanted to talk with you all about in regard to your father's health. The first test we ran showed a tumor enlarged in his prostate that has rapidly spread to some of his organs."

"A tumor?! Is this *something* that can be removed?" Seth asked.

"Unfortunately, no because it's already spread throughout his body...your dad has stage 4 prostate cancer."

"Cancer!" Cynthia shrieked.

My heart started pumping fast. Their voices sounded faint even though I could hear them. It's as if I transferred into another memory. A familiar memory. It was the memory when the doctors came in to tell me that my family died, and I had permanently lost my sight. The sound of everyone was faint beside the beat of my heart and the voice in my mind of the final words spoken by the doctor that my family had gone to. The sound that will forever be plagued in my heart always.

"Yes, and it caused a lot of fluid to build up in his lungs causing pneumonia as well."

"*Like* mama!" cried Cynthia.

"I'm sorry. We're going to do the best that we can. We're going to run some antibiotics through his IV to help clear the pneumonia. And we're going to start treatments to remove the cancer as well as pain medicine. We hope that his body doesn't shut down or respond negatively toward the treatment."

"What kind of treatment?"

"Unfortunately, his progression toward the cancer is severe; we're not able to conduct any radiation or chemo. We can start him on immunotherapy to see how his body responds to that. It can help his immune system to help fight off the cancer. It's a start."

"Thanks Doctor." Zach said.

"I've seen it to where some people have recovery from it. It's a very small percentage, but you never know. Every case can be different sometimes. I will inform the nurses to get started."

The doctor left the room. The sound of the monitor began to beep in my ear again. I heard Cynthia whimpering on the right side of me. I heard Seth's voice, "No, not Daddy" he cried out.

I stood up. I knew the sound came from my left, so I reached out my hand and started walking. My shoes scooted against the floor, and I waved my hand so that I could feel him. I knew I was coming closer because I could hear him faintly. I moved my leg once more, and it brushed up against something.

"Seth?" I called.

He reached up and grabbed my arm to drag me down against him. I wrapped my arms around him as he softly cried on my shoulder.

***

Two Weeks Later

"Our beloved, Stephen Ron Callaway of DeKalb, passed away on Friday, December 8th at a local hospital..."

The funeral had a huge turnout. Everyone came to offer their love, support, and condolences to our dad. There were people whom I hadn't seen since I was a kid. Family, church family, friends, neighbors, people who I had no clue who they were, showed up because that's how special my dad was. Our minister, Eddie Cameron, from the 5th Avenue Church of Christ, was the eulogist. My mom and dad were faithful members of the church since before I was born. I was too until I let work consume me. My siblings and their children sat in the front. Chelsea and I were seated right beside them. She held my hand the whole time. After Paul Taylor sat down from singing the hymn, "*Precious Jesus Hold My Hand*," I went up to the podium to speak.

"For those who may not know me, I'm Seth Calloway, the youngest of the Calloway family. I'm going to read a poem that I wrote for my dad. I want to read it without looking at my paper...but I brought my paper up here just in case I forget the words. I titled it 'Forever, My Dad'." I cleared my throat and read:

If I could turn back the hands of time for Dad, I would

Just to have him for a little while longer

To kiss my beautiful bride on the cheek

To see my kids grow up, to become leaders of this world

To tell me to hang in there because times will get tough

To laugh until we cry or to cry until we laugh

To say over and over how much he loves and misses mama

To hug and comfort us, until we fell asleep

To be that extra prayer when I feel like just giving up

Dad, your love will be forever imprinted on my heart, mind, and soul

And I will cherish you forever

Our bond, will be forever missed

You and Mom rest it up, until we meet again

But for now, I can say, forever my dad

Thank you, God,

Amen.

I walked from the podium and sat down. Chelsea reached for my hand and gave it a squeeze. I smiled.

***

A couple of weeks after my father passed away, I took a leave of absence from my job because I just wasn't ready to go back yet. *I'm without both of my parents now.* I've cried just about every day since he left. I've completely shut out the world right now. I just needed a moment. However long a moment is to get over this pain, I needed it right now. All I have left is just memories. My dad didn't get any better when the doctor first told us he had cancer. He kept getting worse. He went from staying unconscious, to the ICU hooked up on a life support machine. Every organ in his body just completely shut down. I think Dad sort of knew something was going on. I think that he just wanted peace for whatever he was dealing with. He didn't want us to worry. Here I am like the rest of those who miss their parents… alone…even still surrounded by people. There *really* is nothing like your mom and dad. I'm just happy to know he's resting beside Mom. I'm thankful for the love, prayers, and support from everyone. I don't think I would've been able to be *okay* if it wasn't for them…especially Chelsea. I haven't spoken to her since the funeral.

I just need my own time to deal with this.

Only *me.*

I need to go through this alone and just deal with it.

I know next week we are going to meet with our family lawyer to see whatever's left in their retirement. Mom and Dad had a good life insurance plan, so we used the money to pay for all the funeral expenses and the remaining, we just split it between us three. The house and car were paid off. Zachary was living in a duplex so he could take over Dad's home for the time being. He is going to take care of the car in case either one of us will need it in the near future. We also thought about maybe selling the car to someone to put the extra cash into our kid's college fund. It's still just up in the air on that one. I honestly don't care what do with the car. I just wanted it to all be over. I got up, took a shower, and got dressed. I didn't bother eating breakfast or brunch since it was almost noon. I picked up my laptop and sat down at the table to check my emails.

My dad's watch was off to the side of my computer. I picked it up.

My dad's favorite watch as I sat staring at it.

I got up, grabbed my coat, and left.

***

I pulled up to my dad's shop, and to my surprise, I saw Zach and Cynthia's car parked in the yard. This is strange, I didn't expect them to be here, nor did they convey any message to me. I got out of the car. There were only a few cars that were sitting off to the side of the parking lot but those were demolished. My dad kept them just for parts. When I opened the door, on the counter were boxes of Dad's items put in a box. The chairs were all piled together in the corner. Odd, I thought to myself. I didn't think that we were going to do anything else with the shop for the time being. I went back to the back of the shop. My sister's husband, Devin, was here as well, helping Zach empty the drawers to the cabinet. My sister had a rag cleaning off the walls. They didn't realize that I was standing there.

"I guess y'all didn't want to call me to help pack up Dad's items," I said. Even though I showered, I still looked like hell.

"I *did* call you, but you didn't answer the phone. You can grab a rag over there-," Cynthia nodded to the counter, "and help us out. We have to hurry up and clean this place before we put it on the market."

"Who says that we're putting it on the market?" I asked.

Cynthia jerked her head to Zach. "I thought you said that he agreed to put the shop up for sale."

Zach pretended that the conversation wasn't taking place. Or he probably was whipping up a good lie to respond to her. He kept his head down, avoiding our eyes and looking guilty as hell.

"Huh, Zach?" Cynthia was looking at him accusingly.

"No, he *sure* didn't say a damn thing to me!" I said, "I didn't know anything about this." I throw my hands up, looking around the room.

"Look we need to sit down and talk about this," Cynthia said.

"We're family and we suppose to work through this together." "We not selling the shop" I said flatly.

"It's not your decision to make Seth." Zach finally spoke. The prodigal son finally had something to say.

"It is *my* decision Zach just as much as it is yours. In Dad's will, he split his estate between the three of us."

"Yes, and two out of the three are on the same page together."

I look at Cynthia puzzled by Zach's statement.

Cynthia deeply exhaled.

"Look Seth, you *know* as well us that we can't afford to keep this shop, expenses, taxes and all. But I agreed only," she looked at Zach, then rolled her eyes, "if *you* were on the same page with us."

"He didn't want me on the same page with y'all-that's why he went behind my back!" Anger started to rise. "Daddy hasn't even been in the grave long enough and *you* already trying to get his money! You filthy bastard!" I yelled at him.

He started advancing toward me at high speed.

"What the hell did you just call me?! You think you better than me!?

He ran up to me.

"You think you're so bad! You white-collar prick!" He pushed me hard, and I stumbled.

"Y'all stop!" Cynthia shrieked.

I ran up to him and took my first swing, it hit him on the jaw, and he fell down.

"Seth, stop it!"

Then as quickly as he fell, he jumped and tackled me on the counter. He jammed his knee straight into my stomach.

"Ugh!" I gasped out air.

My hands were still clenched to his shirt, and we wrestled onto the floor. He was lifting me up and down, trying to hit my back against the floor, while my hands were to his neck choking the hell out of him. My teeth were clenching as I my hands were getting tighter around his neck. I saw Devin drop down and push his weight on Zach to pull him off me.

"Let go of him, Zach!"

Devin continued to push his weight on Zach, and I felt his grip begin to release.

"Let *go* of him!" Devin shouted as he continued to push, and my hands let go of his neck. Devin pushed Zach completely off of me and he fell on his butt. I got up on my feet. We both were breathing heavily. Zach began to start standing while rubbing his neck. We were still looking angrily at each other.

"I can't believe how y'all are acting!" Cynthia shouted looking at the both of us.

"I don't care no more! I don't care about none of y'all! You have *no* respect for Dad or this family!" I shouted and stormed off. I knocked the boxes of tools off the counter.

***

I was infuriated with my brother! How can you decide to sell the shop and not include me in any of the decisions! Then, to top it off, you deceived our sister into thinking that you did tell when, in fact, you know you didn't. The more I think about it, the angrier I get. I don't know if I'm mad because a part of me *agrees* with them, or I'm just mad because I wasn't able to *take over* the shop. Instead of working overtime at the magazine, I could have been working overtime with Dad, learning about the business.

I *need a drink.*

I'm not an avid drinker-not by a long shot.

But I *needed* something hard today.

"Bottles up Zach."

I've never gotten in a fight like that *ever* with Zach. Of course, we've had our brotherly wrestles but... not to a degree where we just about wanted to knock each other out. Zach was always bull-headed and wanted to do things his way. But *this* was messed up of him.

Snake!

We used to be super close. He was fifteen when his mom passed away. I don't think he's completely healed from that. Or neither have I. We would have gotten the beating of our lives if she saw us fighting like that- even at thirty-five!

I chuckled to myself.

I miss you, Mom! Dad was here to fill in your shoes, but he's not here anymore.

I wiped the tears that streamed down my face.

I turned on the next block. I know where there's a liquor store.

***

Cheers to day number four, I thought as I slowly raised the glass of liquor to my mouth that I had been drinking. I was at home, on the couch, as the music played. My eyelids have drooped on my eyes, and my head feels airless.

I'm beginning to float away, I thought.

And it feels good!!!

I got up and stumbled a bit as I went to the bathroom to take a leak.

I started singing an oldies tune

"It's all right.... It's all right...Have a good time... cause it's all right."

The phone jingled.

"I got SOUL...and everybody knows...cause it's all right," I sang through the phone.

"Bro?! Are *you* okay?!" asked JP.

"Yes," I hissed on the phone, "I'm all right bro!"

"Well, we're about to hit the lounge to catch a comedy show.

Tickets are half-priced since it's in the day. Are you coming man?"

"Yes. I will *be* there." I cracked myself up.

"Okay, man! We'll see you in a bit."

I hung up the phone and drank some more alcohol from the bottle. After the quick gulp consumption, I quickly ran into the room to get dressed.

"Oh, it's all right...."

***

My blanket was snuggled over my shoulders as I sat in front of the electric fireplace by the Christmas tree. I was reading *Pride and Prejudice* while Tamara was upstairs wrapping gifts. She decided to take a day off from work to get started on her Christmas shopping and wrapping. Joseph was at work and Kyla was in school. I had the book opened and my fingers connected to the dots on the page, but I couldn't bring myself to read even beyond five pages, and I had sat there for nearly an hour. I was wondered if Seth was okay.

Why hasn't he called me?

It's been weeks and I'm sure I've left more than ten messages on his phone. I didn't think he would *completely* shut me out. I wanted to be there for him. I *know* what he is going through. I slammed the book together. There's no point in reading this book because I can't focus right now. Maybe I should call him again.

Sigh.

What's the point?

He won't answer it anyway.

"What are you thinking about over there?"

Startled. I didn't even hear Tamara come down the stairs like I normally do. "Nothing."

"Well, I know you're not reading the book because your hands weren't moving when I saw you earlier."

I heard her footsteps come closer to me and I felt her sit next to me. She started rubbing my back. "I miss him, Tam."

"I know you do. Sometimes, guys are very emotional beings, just like us. A lot of times, it's on a deeper level than us. When something hits them really bad, it takes them a moment to come to. Just give it some time, he'll come back around." She assured me.

"Yeah, but I know what it feels like. We can help each other through this together."

"He will in due time. But as he heals, you don't forget to live okay."

Too late! I thought to myself. I only replied. 'I won't."

I know Tamara was probably still watching me. So, I opened back up the book and pretended to read.

"Hey about we go out somewhere-just the two of us. We have a few hours to burn. What do you say?"

I don't know....

Part of me didn't want to go or do anything. But I know Tamara means well and is trying to lift up my spirits.

"Come *on*!" She begged.

"Ok" I gave in. "I know a great spot we can go to!"

"All right let's *do* this *thang*!"

I laughed and got up to get ready.

***

Tamara found a parking garage a block from the lounge. I had to tell her that I didn't mind walking the extra block away from the lounge. I actually loved walking; it helped me to know more about my surroundings. Tamara was super excited about us hanging out. I was too. It's been a while since we really hung out together somewhere. Maybe after today, we can try to do this more often. Since it was cold outside, Tamara had me put on some leggings and a long sweater to go over it with some boots to top it off. Tamara told me she pretty much had on the same attire; it's just our colors didn't match.

"You know I remember coming here once before with a group of girls from college, but I forgot how it looks on the inside."

"Well, how Seth described it-it sounded *really* nice!"

"Was the food good?"

"Yep, I had this Cajun pasta. It was good."

"Did it have a lot of shrimp?"

"They didn't hold back," I laughed.

"Mm. I might try that with a cocktail!" she replied.

When we go inside, Tamara paid for our tickets, and she led me to a table across the door that we came from. The floor felt a bit different from last time, so I know we weren't on the second level.

"Ooh! I like it in here! It is nice! I have to take Joseph to this spot!"

I can hear the excitement in her voice.

"Yes, I loved it when Seth brought me here. Is it a lot of people in here?"

"Yes, it's quite a bit. Oh look, they have a dance floor too!"

"Yep, I've been on it with Seth."

"Look, no more Seth today, okay? This is Lady's Night, and we are doing *our* thang okay!"

"Ok, but you said Joseph's name."

"Ok, that was my first and last time. Now we're even. So, starting now, no more mention of our better halves."

The waiter came over and took our order. Tamara orders the Cajun pasta with a side salad. I was very hungry, so I ordered some Southern Western eggrolls and mozzarella sticks. Today, they have a comedian by the name of Deacon Tarez performing a comedy sketch for us. Some of the things he was saying were pretty fun.

You will have laughter one minute and then roars of laughter the next. He said that he is originally from Chicago but moved here ten years ago to pursue comedy. He said comedy helps him realize that laughter heals the soul. He also said laughter makes you lose weight. So why not have the best of both worlds? We laugh some more. I forgot about the vow that I made to Tamara earlier.

"It would have been nice if I don't want to say his name would have been here," I said.

"Seth!" she said in a faint whisper, like the word just escaped from in her mouth.

"What?"

"Seth is here," she said coldly.

"What?" I had to ask it again.

Did she say Seth is here? *My Seth?!*

"Yes! That's him, he is sitting with a group of people across the other side of the room...Ugh, and he looks a bit rough too! She paused a moment. "Then it's a girl who is all over him-she keeps putting her hands on him."

"How does she look?"

"She's light-skinned with long hair...she looks a bit arrogant"

"That's Kristy," I said with disgust. The anger was beginning to boil up inside me. "I guess he wasn't hurting after all."

"Well, he's about to start hurting! I'll be right back!" The table moved as she jumped up.

"No!" I shouted, "I don't want you going over there!"

She slapped her hand on the table. "Why not Chel?!" she demands, "Something needs to be said! Kristy got her hands all over him and he's not saying *stop*!"

"Please!" I urged. "Please don't go over there! I-I just want to go home."

My heart was beating fast because I thought she might omit what I said and go over there anyway.

Tamara took a deep breath, "Ok."

I got up from the table and she led me outside. I didn't say anything as we were walking back to the parking garage. My jaws were clenched tight. The sadness I felt for him now was anger.

"There's a Walgreens next door. I want to go there to pick up Tylenol and Zyrtec for my allergies. It's probably just another ten-step walk."

We continued to walk until Tamara abruptly stopped. "What the!" she gasped.

She let go of my arm.

"What?! What is it?" I begin to panic again.

"Your picture is on this magazine!!"

"What?! *What magazine!*" I shrieked

"The Majestic...Now he's *really off the deep end!*"

"What does it say?"

"It says, 'A Look Behind the Most Extraordinary Blind Woman, Who Sees Life Through Her Paintings."

I couldn't *believe it!* I thought to myself.

Things keep getting worse and worse.

How could he do this to me?

Not only is he cheating on me, he publicly humiliated me and put my life in a magazine-for the whole world to see!

How can I trust him? Ever again.

***

The wings I was eating had a bit of a kick to them. Whoever cooked these wings put their feet into it. I don't think I've ever had their wings before.

Have I had their wings before? Yes, you had the wings.

I thought I did.

"Seth! Seth!" I looked at JP.

"Why are you looking at your wings like that man?" he asked.

"I was wondering if I had these wings before."

"Dude, you order wings every time we come here. Sometimes you get a twenty-piece or ten-piece wings."

"Yeah, you're right man!" I screamed out and laughed. "I'll take Dad a plate home."

"What?! Dude, you drunk!"

"You're not drunk baby," Kristy interjected. "You just having some fun." She pulled me closer, her arms around me.

"That's right!" I responded. "I'm fun!"

"Well, the show is over now. He was funny." Lizzy said.

"He is doing another here next week. Y'all want to come next week again?" Kristy asked.

"I don't know, we'll see." Lizzy politely said. She stood up to grab her coat.

"Come on man, we'll take you home," JP said.

"No! Y'all go ahead. I'll make sure he gets home safely." Kristy volunteered. "He can finish off his wings."

"They have to-go plates. Come on, man! Let me take you home" JP said once again.

"I want to finish my wings first bro."

"See! He wants to finish his wings. Y'all go pick up the kids." Kristy waved her hands in the air.

"You sure man?" JP asked.

I nodded.

"All right man. Text me when you make home."

JP and Lizzy left the lounge. I continued to eat on my wings and Kristy bought me another drink.

Kristy and I left later that night. Outside the lounge, I stammered to the side of the building because I felt sick, and I was dizzy. I vomited on the ground.

"It's all right, baby," I heard her say faintly. "I'll take you home."

The next thing I knew, I was on the passenger side of my car, and Kristy was driving. "Why the hell are you driving my car?" I asked her.

"Because you were sick, and you felt dizzy. I will make you feel better when we get home." she said to me. I rested my head and closed my eyes.

My eyes awoke when I heard the sound of a car door slamming shut and a pair of heels clicking on the pavement. My passenger door opened, and Kristy helped me out of the car. We were walking up some stairs, and my legs felt so wobbly. I felt unbalanced, like I could easily slip up on anything. My head was spinning all at the same time. I felt like I was in my body then out my body. In and out. In and out. I didn't realize that Kristy turned a key and opened the door. She walked me inside and cut on the lights. I looked all around.

"This ain't my house."

"No, your house was too far away, mine is closer." She pushed me on the couch.

"Let me get you a drink of water. How are you feeling? Does your head still hurt?"

"Yeah."

She came back with a glass of water. I drank some of it and put the glass on the table. She sat on the table right in front of me. I rested my head again.

"Do you have anything stronger?"

"Yes. I have a lot much stronger."

She stood up and slowly walked right in front of me. She bent over and lifted her dress over her body. She tossed it to the floor.

Then she gently climbed on top of me.

"What are you doing?" I whispered.

"Shh," She answered.

My eyes got off focus.

I felt hands lift my head up and I felt lips on mine. My eyes slightly opened. "Chelsea."

"Yes baby, I'm here."

"Chelsea."

"Aw, yes, baby," *she moaned as she kissed me; I* kissed her back hungrily. Her body was moving up and down against me.

Darkness had betrayed me.

And I fell into the thirst of pleasure.

CHAPTER 8

I received another call from a reporter who wanted to meet me so that he could conduct an interview. He wanted to see my paintings. I told him that I wasn't interested and hung up. From that point on, I decided that if anyone else called, I would just let it ring. Tamara, Joseph, and Kyla went to her in-laws for a family gathering and then they were going to go out to eat. They asked if I wanted to go, but I declined. I didn't feel much for being with company. I wanted to spend the rest of my evening painting in the living room. I wanted to bury myself in what I loved best. What I know best.... *Maybe* that's the problem. Maybe he just got bored with me. I wasn't exciting enough for him. Or maybe I was too much of an *extra* load to his daily routine. I keep asking myself *why?*

Why did you want to hurt me, Seth?

Because it was easy,

Because I'm blind and wouldn't know.

I remembered the old saying, "What happens in the dark will always come to the light."

Yeah... but have you ever been blind?

Or "Be careful what you say because there's always someone listening."

But not if that someone is deaf.

And even better, "A person should or shouldn't walk in your shoes."

Maybe they could walk, if they weren't disabled.

I know the logic of those sayings is woven into deeper meanings and factual upon the belief of a higher power.

But what about the physical ailments of individuals that are shadowed by those very sayings? Because our ailments run the deepest.

I continued to paint and then heard the doorbell ring. *Who could be showing up this time of the evening?* I got up and walked steadily to the door with my hands outstretched. The doorbell rang again when I approached the door.

"Who is it?" I asked.

"It's Seth."

My heart sank a bit and then a flow of emotions erupted inside me. Anger was the core but relief and hurt surrounded it-relief that he finally came to me and hurt because I was broken. I didn't know if should open the door. Part of me wanted to close him out forever.

"Hey, you ok in there?" he asked.

I opened the door.

Then I felt his arms wrap around me. I didn't return the embrace.

"I missed you," he said as he kissed me on my lips. My lips were motionless.

Before I could respond, there was a commotion of voices approaching.

"The guys wanted to come see you too. I told you we should bring game night over here."

"Really?" I said sarcastically.

"We brought food and games," JP said as he walked in.

Everyone else followed saying "hello" and small talk.

"Hey, Chelsea." Lizzie reached out and gave me a hug. "How are you doing?"

"I'm okay."

I liked Lizzie. She was warm and friendly. She was quick to reach out to get to really *know me* compared to anyone else out the group. I just didn't like- "Chelsea!"

I knew that voice and smell. It was Kristy. She spoke and even gave my arm a squeeze. "I just love your top!" I heard her walk away.

Relief and hurt were vapor to me right now. Anger had reached the maximum level. You brought this tramp *to my house!*

My nest!

She *knows* where I live now!

And I *sure as hell* didn't know where she stays-*fake skank!*

I walked back into the living with Seth. I don't know how I was looking, but when we sat on the couch he asked, "Are you okay?" he asked.

I didn't respond but chuckled to myself because Kristy sat right beside me.

We played the live-action game of Scattergories. We divided into teams. The other teams have to pick each other's alphabet to use for the topics that we use. The other team also has to pick our topics. One person from each team will have to stand in front and think of a word that starts with the letter alphabet chosen, for that topic. Alex said that each person has 20 seconds to say an answer. JP went up first and we gave him the letter "M" and the topic "A Halloween Costume."

After a couple of seconds, JP yelled "Mummy!" and their team scored a point. We continued to play the game, each of us taking a turn. Even though I didn't want to play, I just did it just because. Everyone else was into it, having fun, and eating on wings. I wasn't. Kristy's turn was next. She was happy and acting like the life of the party. She tried to say something to Seth to add him in on her excitement about the game, but he offered no response. I heard her walk to the front for her turn. The team gave her the letter "S" and the topic "Job Title".

"Mm, that's hard. I can't think of anything that starts with S!"

"Slut!" I blurted out.

Everyone roared with laughter. "What did she say?" she asked.

"Yep, she's right, that can be a job for some people," JP said.

Everyone continued to laugh, but not me.

"I was going to say surgeon," Kristy said. I'm sure her nose was up in the air.

"You took too long to respond," said Alex laughing.

And I felt her sit back down beside me. I got up and went to the kitchen.

I was through for the night, and I wasn't going to go back in there. I couldn't bear it even further with him and her being in my presence and acting as if nothing had happened. I *know* it has! I just have this feeling that something isn't right. I stood there. I knew he was in the room also.

"I've been getting calls from reporters wanting to do an interview me. Why didn't you tell me you were going to *use me* for a magazine, Seth?"

"I *didn't* use you-

"Yes, you did!" I shouted.

I turned toward his direction; anger flared. "You used me *just* for a story! Did you ever sit there- while you wrote the very words I spoke to you and *think* about how I would feel about this? You exposed me!"

"I wasn't trying to expose you! Yes, I *needed* a story for my job, but then I realized that your story needed to be shared, Chelsea!" I felt him walked up closer to me.

"I'm sorry that I didn't tell you upfront what I was going to do. I knew you wouldn't want me to do this, but I had to. You are a gifted person!"

"Gifted! Why Seth?! What?!-Because *I'm blind!* Well, I don't need your pity. I was fine way before you came into my life!"

"No, you weren't! You hid behind your paintings! I wanted to help you see what you were missing out in this world besides not having your sight!"

"I hid?!" I shriek out loudly, "Just like you're hiding things from me."

"What?!"

"I *know* Seth! I was at the lounge yesterday when you were with Kristy and your friends. Is that why y'all here today-to laugh in my face! To laugh and act as if nothing didn't happen."

"We're not laughing at you-"

"Did you sleep with her?!" I cut him off.

A pause.

"Yes, but I was drunk Chelsea! *I wasn't in my right mind!*" I felt his arm grab my arms.

"Let go of me!" I screamed at him. "You *hurt me, Seth!* I *trusted* you! *You* slept with that *slut* and brought her into my *home?! Are you crazy?!*"

"Chelsea, I'm sorry-"

"Get out!"

"Please just *listen to me, let me talk to you-!*"

"Get out!!"

"I *love you, Chelsea*!"

"*Love?*" I choked up with laughter and tears. "*I don't see it because I can't see it, Seth! Love is blind when it comes to me because-I …Can't…See…It! I can never see it! Love was taken from me when I lost my sight…love was taken from me when my family died…love was taken from me when you cheated on me! You don't know what that feels like!*"

"All you care about is your ability not to see! That's all what's built inside-anger for not having your sight! You want me to not see like you! Huh?!"

I heard him storm to the cabinets and pull-out drawers. I heard footsteps running into the kitchen. I heard him scrambling through items. Then I heard him say, "Here it is".

"Whoa, what are you doing with that knife, bro?!" JP asked,

"She wants me to lose my sight, so I will cut out my eyes?"

I felt him walk up toward me.

"I will do it, Chelsea! I swear I will *do it!*"

"Seth! No!" Lizzy screamed out with fear.

I heard her footsteps run up right beside us.

"Argh!" I heard a growling sound through clenched teeth. "*I will do it, Chelsea!*"

I felt his heavy breathing on my face. I heard the tears in his voice. I just stood there silent. Tears streamed down my face. And I was staring right at him.

"Seth-put the knife down!" Lizzy pleaded.

"Seth, you don't want to do this!" JP said calmly.

"Yes, I do! I do bro!" he cried out.

"No, you don't brother! You don't want to do this!" Then as peacefully as JP could say, "What would your father say?"

"He'll tell me not to do it!" He coughed out in tears.

"That's right, he'll want you not to do it. Put the knife down."

Whimpering echoed in the kitchen.

"Put it down," whispered JP.

I felt the heavy breathing start to descend.

Silence

Then I heard the sound of the knife placed on the counter. I felt Seth walk past me. I can hear everyone getting items together and leaving. I felt Lizzy's hands on my shoulder.

"Please leave." I told her.

Her hands fell from my shoulder, and she walked away.

***

I was walking to the car when I heard Kristy's voice yelling after me. I kept on walking. "Seth! Seth!" she cried out as then finally caught up with me. "Are you okay?!"

I turned to her

I wanted her to get the message.

"Kristy, *leave...me...alone okay!*"

"I just wanted-"

I put my hands up, "You just don't get it! *Leave me alone!*" I yelled to her, "Don't ever come near me again!"

I stormed off towards my car, got in, and left her standing there.

***

I stood there alone.

Tears were streaming down my face and my body was shaking.

Anger began to rise up in me, and I started to cry profusely.

Then I made my way quickly to the stairs. I lost my footing and completely toppled over the stairs, landing on my side. I burst out in wails of screams.

"Help me!" I cried out. *"Oh God, help me!"*

I force my body up to continue up the stairs. My hand touched the walls for balance, as I was breathing out heavy sobs. I felt like every breath that came out, only suffocated me more. I wanted to let out every single bit of emotion in me, out. I ran up and burst open the door of my room. I went to every wall in my room and tore the portraits from the walls. I heaved them to the other side of the room. The ones I could tear, I tried. Every single one, even if my hands felt as if they were on fire as I tore apart my pictures. I moved to the bottles of paint and threw them across the room.

"Argh!" I cried out as I threw a bottle against a glass object.

It shattered.

I looked over to the ending wall where I knew what I had to destroy next.

It was the first portrait that I ever painted, the picture of my family.

I stomped toward the portrait and took it off the wall. I tried to tear it, but it didn't budge.

I took in a deep breath and tried to tear it apart again, "*Argh!!!!*" I screamed out as I tried with all of my might.

But it wouldn't.

Not *one* tear.

I was breathing heavily again. Then I heard a sound that filtered into my ears. A familiar sound. A sound that *beckoned* for me to draw to it.

I dropped the portrait on the floor, as I walked toward the sound. I walked slowly out of my room, and slowly down the stairs. My feet carried me through the kitchen and into the living room. The sound grew louder and heavier as I turned the knob to the door that led outside. I walked...and walked...until my feet felt the wet earth beneath them. The pouring rain fell over me, and I closed my eyes to listen to the beat of the raindrops tap my skin. I started crying again because I felt overwhelmed with emotions, and a cathartic feeling ruptured in me. I fell on my knees and lay upon the earth. My head rest upon my arm with tears sliding down my face. I opened my mouth and whispered, "*Lord, help me.*"

The rain continued to fall on me. It was a long moment before I felt strong hands shake my arm.

"Chelsea! Are you okay?!"

"Let me be."

"Chelsea!" Tamara shrieked tugging on my arm, "You will get sick! Now, come inside."

"*Please,* just let me be." I whispered.

I heard Joseph tell her to "Come on baby, let's go inside." Then I felt her arms release from me.

And the rain continued to fall.

I laid in the rain until I knew God heard me.

CHAPTER 9

Two Months Later

The new year was beginning, and I felt the weight of last year was still hunched over my back. I felt alone and empty. Life was still at its continuous, but I was here with no movement. I wasn't happy. I was stressed from working at a job that I was no longer happy with. I was hurt by those who I thought were close to me...and then I hurt the person that I loved the most. Chelsea wouldn't even talk to me. She wouldn't accept my calls, didn't come to the door when I knocked, and she stopped coming to our painting sessions. She completely ghosted me. Absolutely nothing. But who can blame her? I was a drunken fool that night!

One bad decision cost me greatly!

I took in a deep breath and let it out.

Oh, the anatomy of love, I thought to myself. Love is pain but powerful. If love is so strong then why do I feel so empty?

If love is meant to be all these great things, why don't I feel fulfilled inside?

I was interrupted by my thoughts when I heard a tap on my door. I was at the office working on the next issue to go out. I thought work could keep my mind off things a bit-but it didn't. "Come in." I said.

Jacob Manning walked into my office. He was another editor who worked for the magazine. We usually will come together collaboratively and brainstorm ideas to create great articles and ads for the columns. Jacob was tall and a bit lanky. He was a cool, laid-back individual. He's actually a person who I love working with because he keeps me going. There's always that one individual who can keep you at ease when it comes to your job. Sometimes, you are on the brink of putting in your two-week notice, but then that one makes you tough it out just a little while longer...that's Jacob.

"Hey, I didn't want to bother you man, but I wanted to see if you looked over the story that Renee sent over?" He sat down at the desk and handed me the article. "Why are we still single at the age of sixty?"

"That's a really great question. Why is it hard to find love when you're so far into age?" I looked at the written article.

"Yes, she has great content. I think we should publish it. It may not appeal to the younger audience who reads the magazine, but I'm sure the older ones would love it!" He leaned forward and clamped his hands together. "Man, you're into to this pitch I'm spilling to you right now."

"Yeah."

My phone vibrated on the desk. "I am listening."

I picked up the phone, and on the home screen, there was a text from Zach. In the text, it said the property was sold. Tomorrow there will be tow trucks that will move the remaining property.

"I just got a lot on my plate at the moment," I said to Jacob.

I stared at the message. I kept rereading it again. My expression was drawn down, and I was drawn away from Jacob's interaction with me. I felt as if the walls were coming closer on me and every piece of feeling in me was swept away.

"Seth!"

I looked up at him.

"Hey, I know this couldn't be the best time for you. I can't possibly know what you're going through right now. But we have work that we have to get done. A lot of work! Man, you know I'm here for you if you need anything. You know I got you but you have to let me know all right."

I nodded. "Thanks, man"

"No problem. You don't have to get back right with me today about her article-just whenever you can." He rose from his seat. "Hopefully before next month's issue, that is."

I chuckled.

"I've been dealing with some personal issues with my family, primarily myself and this job. "I've just been..." I gazed down for a second, "considering other options. Just looking to see what's best for me and my future."

"Hey, I understand. Sometimes life is better with change." He walked to the door, and then he turned around. "Whenever you get to where you're going in your career, only stop by to bring along me along with you. I know you'll do great."

"I will, man," I replied back to him.

He left my office.

I picked up my phone and reread the text, trying to decide on whether I should respond or not. But I really didn't know what to say from this point. Everything is done. Part of me knew that this was coming. I just didn't expect it to come so soon. I'm sure Zach was doing all he could to hurry up and push the deal from under his belt. Even though I'm a bit pissed about how he handled the situation; I knew it pretty much had to be done. Neither one of us was capable of running Dad's business, nor did we have the inclination to want to do it. That's what hurts me the most, the successor of his property is not his sons...his heirs...it's just a complete stranger. I just hope the property will be treated well.

***

The air was cool, and the breeze was high. We were hoping for snow, but being in the South, the weather can be a bit peculiar. We used to have really cold winters, with a bit of snow here or there. Now, we hardly get snow at all, unless you're maybe in the mountains, of course. I was dressed in a thin sweater, a pair of cargo jeans, and some sneakers. It was the afternoon, and I decided that I was going to go to my dad's shop to bid it farewell. I thought about it last night, and I knew that it was something that I had to do. I had to do it for myself and for my family. I know that this couldn't be nearly as easy for them as well. I would be selfish to think so. I pulled up across the street from the lot. My brother was on the edge of the yard looking at the tow trucks. I didn't see any sign of my sister. I haven't talked to them in weeks since that incident. My sister reached out to me a few times, but I didn't answer. There were some moments I did, but it will be only to pick up the phone to say I am busy and will have to call her back. I never did. I got out of the car and walked up beside my brother.

"The yard is just about cleaned out," I observed. Zach turned to me.

"Yeah, I've been here all morning watching them get this stuff out." He turned his head back to the shop. "I sold it to the highest buyer. Everything should be cleared tomorrow at the bank, so we will split everything amongst us."

110

I nodded.

"What are they going to do with the place?" I asked.

"He wants to just turn it into rental property, maybe build a couple of duplexes or a house. Nowadays, that's all people want to do now, rent out places to make money." He turns back to face me. "Seth, I'm sorry bro...I should have involved you in the decisions. I wanted to take care of everything and that was wrong! Things got out of hand, and it shouldn't have. And I know Mom and Dad wouldn't have wanted that."

I turned to face him. He had his hand out, and I took it. He pulled me into a hug.

"I love you, bro!" He choked up.

"I love you too."

"I don't want us ever to fight again. Okay?" His tears were pressed against my cheek.

"Okay, man." I was still wrapped in his embrace. Zach got emotional, the first time I've seen since Dad's passing. He was hurt just as much as I was. I felt his pain. It wasn't just the deaths of our parents that we've experienced together; it's realizing it's harder experiencing grief on your own. We needed each other. I patted his back.

Zach stepped back and rubbed his eyes. He looked at the shop.

"This is harder than I realized," he said.

"Yeah, I know."

"Y'all make up?" a voice out of nowhere.

We turned around, and Cynthia was walking up toward us. She opened her arms out, and we hugged.

"Oh, Daddy!" she burst into tears.

I kept my arms wrapped around her. Zach stepped in and wrapped his arm around the both of us. We stood there watching the last of the Calloway's establishment come to an end.

***

It's been a little over a week since our dad's shop was demolished. I was feeling a lot better than I was before. The only thing I could do was take it one step at a time. We met with Brent Rowland, the buyer, and finalized everything there that needed to be done in the purchase of my dad's property. It was sold for a substantial amount of money, and after we split it, we each had a good lump sum for ourselves. We've been spending a lot of time this week together, making sure that we all were doing all right. I tried to reach out to Chelsea some more, but it was still a dead end. I wanted to tell her about the important decision in my life that will take place soon...I thought about her all the time.

What was she doing?

What new discovery has she experienced?

Did she still love me?

I just hoped that I didn't break her to the point beyond where she'd given up on everything. Just the thought of that makes a terrible wrench to my stomach. I just hoped that one day she'd forgive me.

I was on my way to meet up with JP at the lounge. It was Friday, which meant poetry night. I had something planned for tonight, so I brought my satchel with me. I also wanted to talk to JP about my upcoming decisions that I made...important decisions. When I made it to the lounge, it was packed; I had to wait at least thirty minutes before I got a table. JP arrived shortly after I got a

112

table. He was dressed in urban attire, with a shirt and a pair of jeans. I opted for a button-down shirt, jeans, and a pair of Gucci canvas sneakers. The waiter came and took our order.

"How have you been doing, man?" I asked, placing a straw in my drink. "Where is Lizzy tonight?"

"She is with the kids at home. She told me to have fun, and drinks are on her."

I laughed. "No drinks for me tonight. No drinks for a long time."

"Yeah, you right! Let's keep it virgin!" He laughed. "How have you been doing? The last time I saw you, it went pretty bad. I do want to say Kristy will no longer be around us; I don't think Lizzy was feeling her like that anyways...neither was I."

"No, no more Kristy." I shook my head. "But I've been doing a lot better. Everything was finally settled with my dad's estate; the property was sold. Zach and I have gotten a lot closer than we were before. So far, everything is working out at the moment."

"What about Chelsea?"

I paused briefly for a second, looking down at the table. "She still won't talk to me."

"You might just have to give her a little more time-"

"It's been weeks!"

"Well, just pray about it. Sometimes prayer is the only option."

"Yeah," I said shortly.

The waiter came with our food and placed it on the table.

"Um...JP, I'm going to put in my notice tomorrow. I will be leaving Majestic by the end of the month."

"That's why you brought me here in public, so I wouldn't cause a scene! You are slick bro! You know, if you would have come to the house, my neighbors would have heard me yelling at you!"

I laughed. "Nall, I got something planned for the night."

"I knew that it was going to come sooner or later. Did you find another job somewhere?"

"No, not yet. I'm not going to be looking for a while either. At the end of next month, I will be leaving for Spain."

"What?! Are you moving there permanently?"

"No. The next few months, I'm going to travel and see the world. My dad and I talked about this for years, and we planned on going together. So, since he's no longer here with us, I decided that I want to venture out on my own."

"Wow, really?!"

JP's eyes were big, even through his glasses. "So, how long will you be gone?" he asked.

"I don't know. I'm just going to go and see where it takes me."

"I'm happy for you man. Really, I am! I think this will be a great opportunity for you, and you need a change."

"Yes, I've been saying that for a while. I need to figure things out."

"Yes, I'm happy and sad at the same time. I won't see my buddy for a while." He picked up one of his wings. "I'm proud of you though. Hey, if I didn't have a family, I'd be right along with you!"

"I'll be back."

"What about Chelsea?"

"It was Chelsea's idea. She said that I should go for it, and I am!

I just got to find a way to win her back."

JP dropped his wing and picked up a napkin to wipe his face. "Look Seth, for her it may have been simple, or maybe easier, for her to fall in love with someone else that is also blind. They would have a much better understanding of each other. But she didn't! She fell in love with you." He used the napkin to wipe his mouth. "You made her experience things that she's never seen before or even thought that she could see. Now, you have to see things on how she sees things... you have to understand her algorithm of being blind and enter into her world. That's how you will ever connect back with her man!"

I let his words sink into my thoughts. "JP, you're a very smart guy. Thank you, man! I'm really going to miss you."

"I'm going to miss you too bro."

We gave each other a fist bump and enjoyed the rest of our meal.

Kenya, the poetry reading's emcee, came to the microphone to introduce the next speaker. She was short and curvy, with dreads extended all the way down to her waist. I think she was maybe the coordinator of the poetry sessions because she was always here. Sometimes, she would come to the microphone and read one of the pieces that she'd written. Her poetry spoke out to me. Her poetry always details such a vivid spectrum of our culture and history.

"I hope you all are enjoying this serene, poetic atmosphere that we have going on right now. Isn't God amazing?" she asked the audience. "He has planted in our souls this inextricable bond of love for those who are willing to accept it." She adjusted the microphone stand to fit her height as she spoke. She looked at her cue card. "Where is Seth Calloway?"

I reached in my satchel, took out a notepad, and got off to walk toward the center of the stage.

"Seth is new to the session. He does a lot of freelance writing in his spare time. He's no stranger to us, he comes pretty regularly.

He said he has a piece that spoke out to all the ladies tonight.

Let's give a round of applause as he joins the stage."

I walked on stage and gave Kenya a hug. I walked over to grab a stool and placed it in the center in front of the microphone.

"Hello, everyone! My name is Seth! I'm going to read a piece that I wrote to all the beautiful women in this room, as well as *all* the beautiful women on this Earth. This piece is very special to me. I have a friend who *inspired me* to write this poem. She's an extraordinary artist, whose paintings go beyond measures. And I hope that one day, you all will be able to see her gifts the way that I do. Her name is Chelsea Davis. And I love her deeply."

I cleared my throat and adjusted the microphone.

"The poem I going to read to you all is titled, "A Portrait of a Woman.":

A woman's art is composed of many colors
Art is her words, music, dance, and culture
Their art is expressed today, yesterday, and tomorrow
It's their imprint from birth that beckons us to follow

Her picture hangs high and is embroidered with gold

A monument she is, sculptured into the perfect mold
Taken from the bone on our side since the beginning of creation
Her sketch of the world is detailed without imperfection

That's why I love a woman

She is gentle as a flower, standing firmly against the wind
She's courageous as a tiger, battling triumphantly till the end
The scars, wrinkles, moles, freckles is the beauty of her skin
The love, warmth, and encouragement is the beauty that's within

Oh, how sweet is her laughter, her voice of affection
Blends melody and harmony, in sweet correlation
Can there be another wisdom that's as wise as she?
Whose words can prick our hearts, like a sting from a bee

That's why I love a woman

The world is composed of many variations of beauty
From His image are you, for you were made for me
Like the slant of her eyes, or a veil-covered face
Or a jewel of her forehead, Native beads design like thread upon
lace

Like the olive of her tone, the pink of her cheek
The salsa of her moves, or the rhythm from her feet
Their sweat, tears, and pain flows like a river to a stream
Their work is never done, and her sacrifice never ends

And that's why I love a woman

I love my black goddess, the Queen upon my throne
From the lightest shade of jasper, to the darkest melanin tone
Her natural beauty glows like the fullness of a moon
She's a work of art exhibit, the main attraction in a room

I love her kinky, curly, coily, afro, twisted, dreaded hair
And the braided, faded, straightened, or all wrapped up to wear
Her skin is smooth and her physique is framed
Like an hourglass figure, her movement ripples like a flame

That's why I love a black woman

Her style is bold and fierce, she can silence a room
She's the spark in a diamond; she's the most expensive perfume
Throughout her struggles, her burdens, her sorrow, unpleasantly words
She's powerful, she'd conquered, she's the history of this world

Black beauty, I love her mind, heart, body, and soul
I love her smile, kisses, and how she makes me whole
You're what we need, God knew from above
Paint her colors over me, the purest of love

I looked out into the crowd. The silence echoed in my ears. I stood up as Kenya approached me. She gave me a long hug.

"That was truly a beautiful poem! It reached me on so many volumes! Let's give this man a round of applause," she said on the microphone.

It was a standing ovation of cheers and claps.

"Seth, you have to come back and read this poem again to us.

We would love to hear again and again"

More cheers.

"You are truly gifted with your words. Women are beautiful and we endure so much. Things can really get hard on us-*especially women of color*. But God placed us here, and our journey is never over. *Now* our hourglass might now be as hourly when we get old..."

Everyone laughed.

"But we still are going to stand. Thank you, Seth, for that beautiful poem! I want a copy so I can frame it on my wall!" "I will" I said.

"I am definitely going to bring you back to read it again and any other poems you write!"

"Thank you!"

I went up to her and gave her a hug. Then I waved and thanked the crowd. "*Chelsea* baby girl, you better come snatch him before I do!" she said.

Everyone laughed again.

*

I was in awe; my eyes began to water. The poem was beautiful! I can hear my cousin and Joseph clapping with the sounds of applause from everyone else in the lounge.

I felt my cousin's hand squeeze my arm.

Aw, Seth!

***

Georgia Academy for the Blind

I pulled my car into the parking lot of a blind school. I knew this would be the answer that I needed to win Chelsea's heart. I got out of my car and walked up to the door. I was going to meet with Audrey Burns. She's been a teacher at the school for years, she even taught Chelsea. She seemed friendly and willing to help me when I spoke to her on the phone. *Here goes faith,* I said to myself and walked into the building.

CHAPTER 10

Three months later

Time had been some since the last time that I heard from Seth. The last time I heard his voice was when he recited his poem at the lounge. The words in his poem still speak to me this very day. I still couldn't get over the fact of how he betrayed me. When I think about that moment, I get angry again. Then I am hurt all over. There's this nick of resentment I feel toward him when I think about it.

What did I do to deserve this?

Or why couldn't you have just walked away?

I asked myself those questions every time when I think of him.

Ever since our fight, I've gotten out of my routine about everything. I hardly ever pick up a brush and paint. Or when I do start painting, I never finish it. I would ask Tamara if a painting looks nice, and she would only say hmm. That's it. Before, I would have heard at least a 'nice' or 'beautiful', or something that was encouraging.

I just haven't been myself, I thought to myself. Maybe I should try something new. Or maybe, I should give Seth another chance... No, maybe I shouldn't.

I was interrupted by my thoughts when Tamara came outside on the patio. "It's a beautiful day out here."

"Is it?" I questioned, merely out of annoyance from being bothered.

"Yes!"

"I have some mail for you. It's from Seth."

"Seth?!" I gasped.

"Yes, Seth! It was mailed here all the way from Spain."

"Spain!?" I whispered to myself. "Open it up!" I said urgently.

I heard her ripping through the envelope. After she finished, she found my hand and placed the letter in it.

"Can you read it to me?" I asked.

"No, I can't."

"Why!?" I protested.

"Because...it's in Braille."

"What!?" the words escaped from my lips. I was in utter shock.

I heard Tamara get up and leave.

My nerves of excitement flush over me. I felt my hands shaken as I felt over the letter. I felt the dots lifted up against the paper. I exhaled deeply. I put in hands in place and began to read:

Hello Chelsea,

By the time you read this letter, I will no longer be in Georgia. I am in the country of Spain. I finally did it! I'm excited and a little nervous at the same time. I am excited because this is something that I've wanted to do for the longest. I call this my T-FAA (I've created a new word), Time-For-An-Adventure. I am embarking on a new journey, a journey on my own. I quit my job, used the money from my dad's estate, and stepped out on faith.

Faith!?

Can you believe that, Chelsea!?

I didn't think I would feel as vulnerable to faith as I feel right now being alone.

It feels great!

I feel new!

I feel different and more alive!

From what I've seen and what I know that I am going to see, I feel humble and blessed.

God has created so much unseen beauty on this Earth, which we as people would hope to see but may never get to experience the moment.

I think to myself, "Wow how immaculate the creation on Earth is- I can't even imagine the glory of heaven!" It goes beyond words.

I am blown away by the magnificent minds, gifts, and talents of individuals, who built, crafted, invented, and sculptured such amazing things-historical things! It's so amazing! You know, this is you too! Chelsea, you have to start your own journey. What makes you so unique is not that you are blind creating beautiful art-that's just the icing on the cake. It's that you used tragedy to create life in your art. That's why you need to get your work out there for people to see...to show the world that you can find the beauty of things even when the worst happens. Death creates Life. You can still push through it because everything will always be all right. That's why I believe everyone should embark on their own journey because you're building a closer relationship with God. It's that one-on-one experience that we need. Having that relationship, you will truly see his magnificent love and power. It truly is amazing!

You're amazing.

Chelsea, I hope that one day you will forgive me because I am truly sorry. I can't erase what happened, but I promise you that I will spend every moment making it right. I know those are just empty words, but you have to open back up to me so that I can show you. Give me a chance to show you.

I hurt you and your family. And I was about to hurt myself in the process that night. I only wanted to inflict pain upon myself because I caused you pain. How stupid of me?

Forgive me.

And if you can't, just think about a tree that's been chopped down and its roots are still alive. All you need is water and the sun to get it back growing. No matter what, I will be that water that flourishes to your roots. And God is the sunlight. It may take some time for the tree to grow, but it will. And when it does...it stands radiantly.

Sometimes it's easier to say forgive and forget. But how often does a person truly do it? You will often hear people say, "I can forgive but I will never forget." But why not?! Because when it's reversed, you would want someone to forgive and forget it too. Then "forget" is not so hard anymore. It becomes easy, and you can move on. Why carry that burden?

Why carry that thought?

We put so much stress on our minds when we can just let things go. I had to realize this because I wasn't forgiving myself. I was in pain from the death of both my parents. I blamed myself, and I shouldn't have...but now I know that I shouldn't, and I can finally move on.

I really did need this, Chelsea. Thank you for helping me to see that.

Spain is a beautiful country. Barcelona has enhanced my world; it has given me words to express on paper. I went to the Casa Batllo, the structure of this building was remarkable, with some parts that looked like bones. I also went to a cathedral that had beautiful stained glass, and high ceilings. It had such a serene atmosphere as I walked on the grounds. It was like a picture out of a magazine. I can't wait to see more of Spain! I will be here for a few more weeks. My address is on the envelope; I'm staying at an apartment in the center of the city. I would love to hear from you Chelsea. But if I don't, then I'll understand. I can only hope.

One day we will come back and share this together.

Love, Seth

***

After I finished reading it, I went back to read it a few more times. I was so happy for him. Reading that letter brought tears to my eyes because I could see how happy he was. I can see how much he needed this. I can't help it but I keep smiling from ear to ear. I feel like I should go out and do something; even try something new.

I laughed to myself

Seth's energy rubbed off on me. I thought, I am ready to get going, now!

I got up from the patio chair and walked inside the house.

But first, I have to write Seth back!

***

I was still in Spain. The Ciutadella Park was beautiful, as I sat there absorbing every scene from all directions. My satchel was laid right beside me as I wrote notes in my journal. It was a low, mild heat but there was plenty of shade throughout the park. I've never seen so much variations of greenery! I thought to myself.

The many shades of green that I've never seen before.

It's incredible!

I sat there a few hours until I got hungry and grabbed a bite to eat. So far, the cuisines here are really good! I went to a local restaurant that's a couple blocks from the rental where I'm currently residing. There are so many different options on the menu, right now, I felt like having this sausage rice dish. I couldn't wait to devour into it. When there's so much walking to do around the city, all you can think about is finding a spot to eat. After I ate, I went to the market to see the many vendors in the area. While I was there, I met a woman named Lucia. She had a vendor who sold her very own spices that she'd grown in her own backyard. There's a Caliente spice that sells out very quickly because a couple of restaurants use her spice for their meals. I brought a few spices to take back home once I leave. She threw in a few extra spices for me to try out. I told her I would share her vendor on my column once I get it started. I also told her that I would stop by soon to visit her. I left and went back home to my rental.

Once I arrived back, I checked the mailbox to see if I received any mail. I unlocked the box and saw a white crisp enveloped addressed to me from Chelsea. I stared at the envelope as my smile began to widen and got wider. I quickly rushed to my room. When

I made it in, I dropped my satchel on the floor and quickly ripped open the envelope.

***

Hello Seth,

I didn't know if or when I was going to ever talk to you. I was trying to rid you off in hopes that you will give up or forget about me.

Because I was trying to forget you...or at least I thought I wanted to so my heart wouldn't hurt anymore.

Your letter reached out to me in so many ways. I finally can read your words on paper! You touched my heart deeply as I read it.

Your words!

I must have read your letter about a million times!

Well, I don't want you to get the big head, so let's just say a couple of times!

I'm so proud of you! You went out there to seek the journey that you always wanted. I commend you for that. I think I will use the new term you created, T-FAA. I am going to embark on an adventure here as well. You inspired me to do so. I spoke to Mr. Chaplin, and we're going to discuss what paintings I'm going to sell and the pricing. We pretty much want to just put my paintings there and see how it goes. I haven't been in the studio in weeks prior to the incident. I tried to avoid any means of running into you, and the other part of me, I'd lost myself completely. I lost my zeal for art. I lost the zeal within myself. I was just...here.

Your letter was the message that I needed to hear.

127

Slowly I'm getting back to doing what I love to do. I told myself that I could do more than just paint. I AM more than just being blind. I never thought I felt that way about myself until I met you.

Thank you for helping me to see that, Seth.

In your letter, you ask for me to forgive you.

I do forgive you, Seth.

But it will take time for me to give you back my trust. It's not as easy to forget, but I will spend every moment trying to. That's the only way that I know I can heal from this...is time. I'm glad that you took responsibility for the matter. I know Kristy definitely played her role as well. I think what hurts the most for me is that I don't think you would have ever told me if I hadn't known.

That's something that I just hadn't gotten over with yet.

After I write this letter, I'm going to paint under the moonlight. I love painting under a full moon. I can do a sunset or a sunrise. But it's nothing like the moon. I love a full moon. The air is different. It's calming and serene. And even though I can't physically see the glow of its light, I can feel the glow radiate from my skin. I can paint under the glow of a moon for hours.

Whenever you have a moment to see a full moon outside, go outside and appreciate it. I want you to take out your journal and write. It will change your life forever.

I'm glad that you are enjoying Spain, its culture, food, and people. You are experiencing a new world that I only wanted to hide from. Exposure I thought would only cripple me further. But I was wrong. Being different is not being hidden in the darkness, but a friend to shed light. Maybe one day I will get to share that *adventure with you. I know your dad is looking down at you smiling and saying, "That's my son, he did it!" ...And you did Seth! I want to tell you what your dad said to me one day when you were making us a sandwich in the kitchen. I told myself that I wouldn't tell you until I knew when the time was right. He told me that I got myself a good guy. I asked him, "How so?" He said, "Because I raised him!" and I laughed. Then he touched my hand and said, "Because he's never met anyone who rides the waves even when it's steady." At the time, it took me a moment to fully understand what he meant. But now I do. You're doing it now, and you were doing it when I first met you. You find the adventure in everything you do, even if you're by yourself. You have to be different from the rest, and that's such a good thing. That's what made me so attracted to you in the first place. You treated me not as a blind person but as someone who is normal. I forgot how normal was since my family's death. I spent the years after blaming myself for what had happened. If only I didn't beg my dad to go see the lights that night, we could have been at home. I lost faith in God for years, and I blamed him and everyone else in my life. I felt life wasn't important for me anymore if all I'm always feeling is sadness, anger, and loneliness.*

Then, I, too, had to forgive myself.

I easily gave up on Him when he's never once given up on me.

How selfish was that of me?

The greatest gift God had, he gave it to the world.

The family I had, I wanted to keep them to myself.

I had to realize that they never belonged to me in the first place. I was finally at a place where I felt good about that. I was finally at peace within myself. Love is about letting go and letting God.

I couldn't have done that without you. God places people in our lives for specific purposes. Now, we share something in common: our parents' demise. He brought us together at the right time. He knew we would have to lean on each other. I told myself that I would get better with my spiritual life, and that's going to be one of the new changes that I will be making. I hope you enjoy every moment in Spain, and I look forward to hearing about the next adventure that you have in store to visit. I hope you take lots of pictures so that I can see them in you. Remember, you are not alone.

Chelsea

***

Hello Chelsea,

After two months of Spain, I've ventured into new territory... Greece!

I figured I would at least stay in each country for a couple of months. I want to dive into the cultural stance of each country. The first couple of weeks were a little rough with my rental. I actually had to cancel my first rental because it wasn't well-kept at all. The cleaning crew didn't do a good job at all. The sheets were filthy and used towels were still laid on the bathroom floor. So, I had to check into a hotel for the night and rent another apartment. This new rental really compensated for what I saw at the previous one. So far everything is going well. Greece is just absolutely breathtaking! From the structure of the houses to the beautiful beaches and the landscaping, Greece is quite cultivating. Just a couple of days ago, I went to see the "Acropolis," and the view of this architectural monument was striking. As I stood on the grounds, I felt like I was a part of the ancient civilization that rested here centuries ago. Believe me when I say that I felt the ground move beneath my footing.

It was super surreal Chelsea-and a bit chilling!

I didn't know what to take from it-was it just a tremor of an earthquake or the lingering spirits of its territory. I know I wasn't going crazy because there were a couple a few diameters from me, and they felt the tremble too. I took it all in and silently said a prayer. I find myself in prayer more now than I've ever had in the past. I felt like my connection to God has gotten stronger and I feel closer to him. I had a moment the other day when I was thinking about my mom and dad. I just started crying.

Like the tears continuously flowed from my eyes and I couldn't stop it.

I miss them so much!

When you're alone, a lot of things always cross your mind. Lately, it's been my parents...and you. At one point, I was about to take a flight back home. Then I thought about it. I thought to myself that I couldn't allow depression, anxiety, and fear to over-whelm me. Because if it does, I become a shadow set apart from my inner light. And I can't allow that to happen. So, one night, I took your advice and went outside to watch the moon. It wasn't full yet, but I definitely will sit outside when I see a full moon as I travel from country to country. As I set to watch it, I did admire it. It is amazing how something that seems to be small and millions of miles away can light up every surface of this planet. It really does have this serene presence and energy. I actually took out my journal and started writing in it.

Thanks, Chelsea, for forgiving me.

I hope a lot of doors open for you in time to come. When they do open and they surely will, I want you to take the most of every opportunity because you deserve it. I think having your own art studio will be a great opportunity for you. Make sure to save a ticket for me because I can't wait to see what you have in store. Maybe one day you can paint a portrait of me-hint. I'm sure there will be quite a bid on it!

Tomorrow, I got a lot of things planned. I will be going to a dance festival, and I am going to visit the Temple of Zeus. So tomorrow will be more walking. I lose weight by doing a lot of walking but I gain a lot by doing a lot of eating. Isn't that something?

Talk to you soon,
Tell everyone I said 'Hello.'
Love, Seth

***

Hello Seth

The family told me to tell you "hello" as well, and I hope that you are having fun. I have some exciting news! I've recently gone back to the art studio to continue my sections. I gave Mr. Chaplin the thumbs up to sell my paintings because people have been inquiring about them. Soon after, I received a call from Daniel Galenski, one of the most renowned artists of this time, called and said he would love to buy some of my portraits!

Can you believe it?

I was just speechless.

So come to find out, he is actually an acquaintance of Mr. Chaplin. He's been wanting to purchase one of the paintings for some time now. Apparently, he has a house here in Georgia, so when he is in the city, he sometimes stops at the studio. Mr. Chaplin told him that I wasn't selling my paintings at the moment and Mr. Galenski said for Mr. Chaplin to give him a call if I ever decide that I do want to start selling my paintings. So, he called, and we met up. He purchased my paintings for a good substantial amount of money.

And get this?!

He wants me to paint of portrait to hang in his office that he has in New York! He also wants to fly me out to his art studio so that I can see his gallery. Of course, the family is going to come with me. I'm just super excited! He was super nice and sweet. He is also going to refer me to some of his colleagues who also have a fascination with art. Seth, from what I earned from the paintings I can finally open my own art studio. I talked to Mr. Chaplin about it, and he thought that it would be a great idea also. I'm super excited! I am finally stepping out and creating my own journey. A local reporter, Rachel Zegler, came to the studio to conduct an interview with News 11. I was a little nervous at first, but I thought that now was a better time to show a little of myself to the world. I told her I would only answer a few questions. I told her I already had someone in mind that I would open up to completely...

His name is Seth Calloway.

So, Seth, whenever you get your own magazine-and you will! I would be happy if you would interview me. I wouldn't want to have it any other way. I only hope that you are still interested in my story. I know that whatever you write, it will be grand. You have a way with words in how you use them and say them. You are meant to write! That's why I am glad that you are embarking on seeing many different lifestyles and creations. How else can we hear about it?

Who else can give us that raw, honest, relatable information? Only you...

Your words are so impactful, that I willingly gravitate to whatever you write. I know you're hurting right now. There are still times when I think about my parents, or some feeling that I have will cause me to cry. And it's ok to cry. I don't want you to give up on this. You don't know how many people would love to be able to do what you are doing right now. I am one of those people. I would love to be out there enjoying every moment. I would probably be getting on your nerves because I would want you to describe everything that you are seeing. I'm sure you will have loads to write about. For the people you meet out there, you can be their voice to share with other parts of the world. You can be their connection to expand their vision to the world.

Because that was what you were trying to do with me, and I didn't give you that chance.

I hope that you will continue to enjoy the many attractions that Greece has to offer. Right now, it's the summer and Georgia is extremely hot. Joseph has been doing a lot of grilling outside, I am almost tired of eating ribs and BBQ chicken. I am almost completely burned out of the whole thing. I laughed at your letter when you talked about making a portrait of you. You have my word; I will give it to the highest bidder. So far, the highest bidder may be Kyla! I would buy it, but water painting isn't hot on the market right now. Mr. Galenski might think it belongs to one of his kids!

Ha ha!

Sometimes I just crack myself up!

I also wanted to let you know that I got approved to start teaching a session of art at the blind school. I might just do a couple of sessions a week for those students that are interested in art. I'm super excited about that as well. Everything hasn't been written in stone yet, but I will let you know once I finally get the confirmation about everything. Until we talk again

Chelsea

***

Hello Chelsea,

I am in Italy! This was definitely on the top of my list because I couldn't wait to see the Colosseum! And let me tell you, it was immaculate! The history of this world goes beyond measure. It never ceases to amaze me how people used their minds and hands to build beautiful landmarks. Sometimes, you just have to look at it and take it all in. I do know one place that I am going to take you when we come back here. I am going to take you to the Sistine Chapel. It is a mural of paintings that are displayed on the walls and ceilings. It makes you wonder...

How was this man able to paint on these high ceilings, beautiful artistry?

And...

For the abundance of beauty on this Earth, why don't we have that abundance of love with each other?

And I think about how every person has that favorite color or colors that they love or think it's beautiful...

But why can't we love the many colors of someone's skin?

Why can't the world have that perception of all colors being beautiful?

Then, the world would become a better place... and our eyes would be open to God's creation in the rarest form.

His paintings made me think of you and how you paint such wonderful pictures. I thought about how you use your colors to create meaning behind each piece. A picture of flowers in a vase to us would be flowers in a garden to you. When I think of colors, I always think of you.

Italy will be another on our bucket list. The food and people were so pleasant. I met a guy named Antonio who owns a restaurant. I don't remember his last name, but I will forever remember our interaction. When I come back to Italy, I will come to his establishment. I told him if he was to come to the States, he was more than welcome to stay with me. He owns a restaurant on the outskirts of the city. It's a very popular restaurant that everyone goes to because the wine is exquisite. It really is the best wine I've ever tasted and I'm not a big wine drinker at all. The restaurant is only open on the weekends because, on the weekdays, he is busy making his wine. He owns a small family vineyard, and they process the fruit to make wine. He also exports his wine to his family in New Jersey because they have a restaurant out that called Gallo's Italian Finest. His wine is always in high demand so he stays pretty busy. A tenth of what they earn, they make sure the proceeds go to many outreach organizations and charities. Antonio is a very cool, nice guy! I can see why his business has thrived in the many years since it's been opened. In the short time that we conversed, he has a lot of love and passion for what he does for his family and the citizens of Rome. He reminded me of my dad. Two of many I aspire to become.

I have two more countries to visit. It's all going so fast. The word "amazing" will always flow from my lips as I travel to these countries. I hope to hear from you soon.

Love Seth

***

Hello Seth,

I am happy that you are doing extremely well out there visiting the beautiful countries. I hope you're taking advantage of the camera I got you, taking lots of pictures. The year is almost winding down. We just came back from a beach vacation. We went to Destin and stayed the weekend on the beach. It felt so nice. The breeze from the water and the waves brushed against my feet. I wanted to stay another week! Of course, Kyla will be starting school soon. Speaking of school, I will be teaching every Monday, Tuesday, and

Friday out of the week for a couple of hours a day. I started a couple of weeks ago, and the kids were great! They participated and were very eager to want to paint. When they leave, they always give me a hug and say, "Thank you, Mrs.

Davis." It makes me so happy that I can make a difference in their lives. I want them to teach them that they can do anything. On Fridays, I teach the audit classes.

I told you before that I was going to start my new venture. The new venture is music! There's a music teacher whom I befriended by the name of Heather Perry, who has been helping me with playing the piano. I've been wanting to play a musical instrument for some time now and I finally did it! Heather's classroom is just a couple of doors down from my classroom. I heard a beautiful sound one day and I went to see what it was. Heather is a very sweet and intellectual person. She can tell you about anything. She's not blind but she wanted to teach at a blind school because she felt that she would get the most out of her teaching. She said she loved helping those who are in need of something special because they are special.

Isn't that wonderful?!

I just love to hear her, and the students play the piano. I'm okay at the moment, still new to the area of musical instruments. She did say my form is great on how I press on the keys. I'm going to take that compliment and keep on practicing. Heather has helped me a lot at the blind school. When I teach, she will come in there sometimes and be my assistant. She's bought one of my paintings as well. I actually donated one of my portraits to the school. This school helped me along my journey as a blind student. I want to help out too.

Italy, by far, seems to excite you in numerous ways! I loved how you dived into the art of colors with the mural paintings that you saw on the walls-beautiful Seth!

And I loved how you used colors as a representation of how we should view ourselves as people of this world...in love...the love of many colors.

I like the sound of that!

Thank you, Seth, for always sharing! I will talk to you soon.

Your friend,

Chelsea

***

Hello Chelsea,

I'm in the most romantic city in the world...Paris! Paris definitely is a city of love. In the package I sent to you, you will see that I gave you your Christmas gifts a little early. The scarf is from a store that I saw in town. An Asian lady owns the shop and she handmade every fabric that's detailed in the scarf. She also sells articles of clothing as well. I thought it was so neat, her fabric was really nice. Her name was Atta. If I was still working at the Majestic, I would have loved for her to be in my column. That is true talent, and she's created her own sense of fashion.

Some fabrics have patterns and solid colors that I've never seen before in the new era of fashion! I hope you love the scarf. When I saw the pattern and colors, I knew I had to get it for you.

Hopefully this year, Georgia will have a lot of snow.

The second gift I gave you is a promise key. I want to make a promise that we will come to Paris together one day and throw the key over the bridge into the river. I wrote our names on a yellow ribbon, tied the ribbon to the locket, and placed the locket on the bridge. I know its exact location when we return to the spot together.

Since Paris is a romantic place, I had to reserve our spot. I love you, Chelsea! You're the woman that I want to spend the rest of my life with. I want us to grow old together. I want our kids to run around the house knocking over bottles of paint and scribbling on my notebook. I want us to watch every sunset, sunrise, and full moon together. I want to kiss you over and over again and explore every single part of you. We can have our journey with God as the centerfold of our lives. I need you, Chelsea.

Who else can narrate my story?

Taking this journey alone not only built my relationship with God, but it helped me to grow as a man, as a person, and as a Christian. Any journey partaken will always equal growth. You help changed me... You!

I must say that I'm really not doing as much in Paris; I'm mostly eating and taking in the views. Right now, I am sitting in front of this charming castle and writing this letter to you. In this city, I want for us to experience things together, so I am going to omit going to the big attractions. This is definitely worth waiting for if I have you in it. I hope I didn't come off too strong, but I had to let you know how I felt. My words are binding since it's on this letter.

Ha ha!

Love, Seth

***

Hello Seth,

Love is a powerful feeling. It's meant to be genuine and uncon-ditional. It's meant to be a vow not broken. It's a faith unyielding; and a hope yearning. Love is kind, patient, courageous, and forgiv-ing. Love is free and willingly leads us in the right direction.

We should have that love for one another.

We should have that love for each other.

I'm glad that you shared your feelings. I only apologize that I'm not as forward. You're the first person that touched me so deeply. So intimately. This is new to me. I was a fragile, broken girl that has experienced love on many levels...

I just don't know...

I'm a little afraid.

I sent you a gift, and I packaged it really tightly because I don't want you to open it until Christmas next month. Please don't open it until Christmas. It was something that I had to give you because it reminds me so much of who you are. I think you will like what I got you. You know I love the holidays, especially Christmas. This year, I am going to go all out for it. I am going to do a gingerbread house, tour the neighborhood lights, and partic-ipate in the Christmas pageant at our church. I plan on having the kids decorate stockings for Christmas. I've gotten better with my piano lessons; maybe when I see you, you will hear one of the pieces I've been practicing on.

I have some exciting news! Tamara is pregnant with baby num-ber two! Kyla is going to be a big sister! She's just a couple months in but I think she's going to have a girl-her mood is already through the roof!

Ha! Ha!

The next exciting news that I wanted to share is…I found an art studio! Mr. Chaplin is going to be working with me. He is going to sell his studio and be full-time with me. In the next couple of weeks, we'll be moving items to the new studio. It's bigger than what Mr. Chaplin had, and there's a room that he can still use to teach art. I'm still selling a bit of my portraits-all thanks go to you, Mr.

Chaplin, and Mr. Galenski. I'm super excited! This is what I have been dreaming my whole life and now it's came true. I am truly thankful!

I miss you, Seth!

Yours truly,

Chelsea

***

Hello Chelsea,

Thanks for the gift! I love the portrait! It took a lot out not to rip open the gift, but I held out. I told myself I had to do it for you because I know how much you love Christmas! I love how you have me looking at a picture with a reflection of an elf. I don't know how you create the pictures that you make; I can only say God knew what he was doing. I remember you once told me that elves are helpers. I know now why you sent this to me.

Thank you!

I will hold this picture forever.

I am in London right now, the final stop of my adventure. London is a really cool place! I haven't gotten into much of the extractions yet, I'm just soaking everything in at the moment. I just want to blend into the culture here. Of course, that is the bare minimum because I don't have an accent.

Ha Ha!

I really stick out in the crowd.

I have to get used to the tradition of taking a very long break every day to drink tea, rest, hang out, and do other things. In the States, I'm used to only taking a thirty-minute break, and that's if I can. But I like the long breaks. It gives you more time to relax and revamp.

Sorry, it's been a while since I've written to you. I've been a little busy adjusting to life here in London. We are already well into the New Year, and I've started off really well. I got a job! I know you're probably thinking- What?!

But yes, I wasn't thinking about wanting to work, neither was I trying. I was offered a job because I frequently would visit this tea shop. I'm not a tea drinker...well I wasn't until I started going to this shop and now, I really love tea! The tea they sell is so good! They also serve brunch items here as well as pastries. I just fell in love with the establishment; the atmosphere is wonderful. It's a family-owned business. The owner is my friend Paul. Paul is always short on help because the workers always leave. They leave because they don't want to work or they get bored. We started talking one day because he noticed that I kept coming in and we just vibe. He offered me a job and I accepted. I told him it was only temporary. He said that I could work for him- which doesn't pay as much, and he would offer me free room and board. I thought that it was a great offer. I can save some and not use any of my money. Paul is really good people; his family is nice as well. The shop is in town but they live on the outskirts in a nice little home. Paul has a wife and two kids. His wife Chloe, used to help him at the shop when she could, but the kids demanded more of her to stay at home. Paul prefers it that way anyway.

Chelsea, I told him I would stay temporarily...but I really don't know how long that will be. Part of me wants to come back home and the other beckons me to stay. I will come back home only for you...only if you want me to. Europe captivated me in a lot of ways...but only you captured me.

My journey ends with you, only for our journey to begin. If I receive a letter from you then I will take the next flight out...

And if not,

I will stay in London.

Love always,

Seth

CHAPTER 11

Today was very warm, and the feeling of spring was about to start. I recently got home from my early piano lessons. I pretty much know the letter keys and the sound of each one. Heather had me practice playing chords from a stream of melodies that was heard from a music speaker. I'm not on the road to being a pianist. It was just one of those things that I always wanted to learn to play. I wondered if Seth knew how to play the piano, or even know how to sing. I will ask him that in the next letter that he sends me. *He's been gone for months, and I feel lonely as ever.* I thought to myself. *I knew this was something that he needed...as a writer and as a person.*

I was interrupted in my thoughts when my door burst open. I heard quick footsteps and Kyla leaped onto my body.

"Guess what auntie?!" she exclaimed. "Mommy is going to ask if you can watch me so Mommy and Daddy can have some alone time!"

"Ouch! She is- is she?!" I asked rising from my bed. I felt a sting of pain hit my stomach because Kyla jumped on me. I heard Tamara's soft footsteps walking toward my room.

"Kyla! Go and clean up your room!" Tamara informed her.

"I *did* clean up my room."

"No, you didn't, there's still some toys on the bed. Now go clean them up!"

"Ok" as her footsteps stomped out of the room.

"Doesn't sound like she was too happy to clean her room?" I said with humor.

"Neither was I when I *looked* at her room." I felt Tamara sit right beside me.

"Miss Eavesdropper is right, do you mind watching her while Joseph and I go out for dinner?" she asked.

"I heard that!" Kyla shouted from her room.

"Clean your room!" Tamara shouted back.

I laughed. "Of course, I will!"

"Thank you! We want to spend a little alone together before little one comes." Tamara grabbed my hand and placed it on her stomach. 'Do you feel that?"

I laughed. "He must be hungry."

"He must be!" she laughed.

"I can't wait to meet him!" I was rubbing her stomach.

"So, you think it is a boy?" she asked.

"Maybe, you don't seem to have any pregnancy whoa compared to Kyla."

"I haven't! This has been an easy pregnancy."

"Kyla will be such a big helper," I assured her.

"Yes, she will," I felt Tamara squeeze my hand, "How have you been doing?"

"I'm doing good! This year has brought out so many opportunities and blessings. I can't thank God enough for all he has done and continues to do. I'm so thankful. I just hope it stays that way."

"And if it doesn't Chelsea, we still need to be thankful even when the storm comes. Just like any storm, it doesn't last always," she assured me, "The calm always comes after the storm...storms help build our faith in God. That's where we find our strength." She wrapped her arm around my shoulders. "We can't have faith in him only when good things happen or when good things come our way. We have to be thankful to God even in the bad because he who helps will always cometh."

"Yeah."

"I know you miss him. And I *know* you love him. Don't let one mistake deter you from happiness. Whether it's Seth or someone else, move on to be happy within yourself, life, and family." I felt her get up from my bed.

"I'm going to start getting ready. Before we leave, I will take the lasagna out of the oven for y'all to have dinner later."

She left and I sat there. I wondered if I was ready to let it go.

Two hours later, Tamara and Joseph left for their outing. I walked down the hallway to Kyla's room. I heard a clicking sound.

"What are you doing?" I asked.

"Nothing, I'm just playing with my dolls. Hey-can I watch TV?"

"Hmm, we'll watch some TV after we eat."

"Yes!"

"I'm going to jump in the shower right quick and after that we can eat."

"Okay."

She ran up to me and gave me a hug. "I love you."

"I love you too. You continue to play, and I will jump in the shower."

"Okay."

I smiled and heard her footsteps run back to wherever she had left. I turned around and walked back to my room to shower.

***

I slowly crept down the stairs. I heard the sound of water. Chelsea is still in the shower. I'm tired of playing with Barbie dolls. I want to draw some pictures. There was paper on the floor. My drawings were where I left it this morning. I ran to my crayons to begin coloring. I pick up the pink crayon so I can draw a flower and a picture of Mommy and Daddy. I will surprise Mommy and Daddy with my picture. I started humming the tune to Dora the Explorer.

"*Come on, vamonos,*" *I sang,* "*everybody, let's go*-Mommy is going to love this picture! She loves flowers and the smell."

I looked at the table and saw a candle with fire. "Wow!" I whispered.

I walked to the table and watched the candle. The fire danced and glowed before my eyes. I picked up the candle and placed it on the floor with my pictures. I just watched it glow. I reached my arm out to touch it- "Kyla!" *Bang!*

The candle fell on the papers and the fire struck it.

"Oh no!" I gasped.

I stood up and ran up the stairs.

***

"Kyla!" I yelled again as I was putting on my shirt.

I heard her footsteps run into my room "Yes, Auntie."

"Where were you? I called your name twice."

"I was coloring downstairs."

148

"You know you're not supposed to go downstairs without me."

"I'm sorry. I just wanted to draw."

"Ok, we will color in a moment. Now go into your room and I will get you when I am finish."

"Auntie…"

"Yes."

"Never mind."

I heard her footsteps walk away.

I walk into my room and lay on the bed. I lay thinking. Then I closed my eyes…

…What seemed like a dream of Seth resting his hand on my face, gazing into my eyes, and leaning in for a kiss. It turned into a nightmare quickly! His pupils darkened, and he was no longer looking into my eyes. He was looking over my shoulder. He screamed out my name. I turned my head over to see where he was looking, and fast approaching was a thick cloud of smoke.

I screamed and woke up.

I coughed.

My nose flared to the reality of smoke that lifted into my nostrils.

Cough!

It was strong. Something was wrong, something didn't feel right.

Is the house on fire?

"Kyla!" I screamed. I had to get to her fast. "Kyla!" *Cough.*

No response.

I leaped off my bed and quickly began to walk outside the room. I continued to call, but there was no response. *Oh God, please don't let anything happen to her. Help us.* I silently prayed. My heart was racing, and fear had already flared inside of me. I felt intensely hot and sweat began to drip from my face.

"Kyla!! Where are you?!" *Cough.*

Every time I screamed, the smoke I inhaled burned against my lungs. I made it to her room and felt around the familiar wall. I lifted off the wall to find her bed in the center. I felt around her bed and fell to my knees to feel under the bed. Under the bed is usually where she goes when we play hide and seek. I stood up with my hands and reached out to feel around every square of her room. I went back out in the hall to move toward Tamara's bedroom.

" Where are you, Kyla? Please tell Auntie! Kyla!"

I went into Tamara's room quickly checking what I could. I started to cry out. She was nowhere in their room.

Crash!

I heard the sound of glass shattering from a window. I have to check downstairs. I walked outside the room to quickly walk into the hallway. The smoke was getting denser. I knew that there was a fire somewhere but where?! I placed my hand on the banister.

"Eek!" I screamed in pain. The banister was scorched with heat. The core of the fire had to be downstairs. I can feel the thickness of the smoke and the blaze of the heat on my skin as I walked down the stairs. I was on the next to the last step when my foot hit something hard, and I tripped over, toppling on the floor.

Uff.

The wind was knocked out of me and my head slammed on the floor.

"Ahh," I moaned in pain. *"Kyla!"* My head throbbed and there was a sharp pain in my shoulder. My foot still was on top of her. I scrambled up to her. I shook her body. No response. The crackle of fire around us, and the smell of smoke worsened. I was coughing more. I knew I had to get us both out of the house; luckily the stairs were close to the front door. I reached out to pick up Kyla. I winced from the pain in my shoulder, but my adrenaline overshadowed the pain at the moment. I had to let God by my eyes now. I lifted her into my arms, she felt light as a feather. I don't know if it was my adrenaline or she's gone. I staggered to the door. My knees felt like they wanted to buckle over from the pain when I fell on the hard floor. Pain ripped through my body, and I collapsed over Kyla. My cough burned my throat, and my lungs felt heavily inflamed. I used the last of my strength to push myself from Kyla and rose from the floor. When I reached the door, I dropped on my knees. I screamed out in pain. I felt for the doorknob and quickly opened the door. I lifted Kyla high up against me and walked into the night.

"Help me! Help me!" I screamed out so that the neighbors could hear.

I kept walking until I knew I was far from the house and fell on the ground. I lifted my hands to Kyla's face and began to shake.

"Kyla!"

I lifted her up to my face to see if I could feel a breath, but I couldn't. "Kyla!" I began smacking her face.

"Kyla!" I choked out a scream when I heard a soft moan. "I'm sorry," she said in a faint whisper, "I didn't mean to."

"*It's all right, Auntie is her-* I choked out a cough. I kept coughing and fell back hard against the ground. I was out.

***

Beep Beep Beep

I slowly opened my eyes to the sound of the machine that was beeping right beside me. I slightly moved my hand to feel the bed pressed underneath me. My hand felt like a bandage was wrapped around it. It was still throbbing in pain. I knew I was in a hospital bed. My head was hurting really bad.

"Chelsea?!"

I can hear the sound of Tamara's voice.

"Tamara," I whispered.

"Hey Chelsea, how are you feeling?"

"Kyla?!" I projected out, "How is Kyla?"

"Ssh." Tamara touched my arm and was rubbing it. "She is fine. You saved her life. The doctor said if she would have stayed in the house a moment longer..." Tamara paused to find her wording, "she wouldn't have made it."

"Is she awake?"

"Yes, she suffered a few minor burns, and her lungs were impacted by the smoke. Everyone is fine now. You guys will be here for just a few days with round-the-clock treatment."

"*Me?*"

"You're the same as Kyla. You did suffer a slight concussion. You've been out for some hours; they had to closely monitor you.

They have you on pain medicine because of the pain in your head.”

“Yes.” *The fire!* I remembered Kyla’s last words spoken to me. “The fire-*Kyla* said that she didn’t mean to do it.”

“Yes, Kyla knocked over a candle jar. I forgot to blow out the candles before we left, a *mistake* on our end. I apologize for that. She was just afraid to tell you.”

A feeling of remorse swept over me. Tears welled up in my eyes and before I knew it, I was crying.

“Ooh!” Tamara called out, and I felt her arms wrap me up in a hug.

“Ssh! It’s okay! She rubbed her hand up and down my back. “Ssh, everything is fine! It’s not your fault. It was an accident.”

“You should be with Kyla.”

“No!” she said firmly. “I’m going to be here with you. Joseph is with her and Kyla wanted me to stay with you to make sure *you* were all right.”

“I feel like things always happen to me! When things go good, then it goes bad. I just feel so tired...I’m tired. I feel like no matter *what* anyone says, I *still* feel alone. One day I’m fine, and then the next, I’m not. I *hate* feeling like this! I don’t *want* to feel like this!”

I felt some discomfort in the back of my throat because I was just highly emotional. I couldn’t stop crying. It wasn’t just the incident that occurred that got me so emotional. It was the trauma that I went through when I was a child. A trauma that I psychologically haven’t dealt with since it happened, it has carried with me through these years.

"Chelsea, the reason why you keep feeling like this is because you are keeping everything suppressed inside of you. It's not meant for us to go through depression and anxiety on our own. That's why we have God...our family, church family, friends, doctors, and those who can help, love, pray, and support us when we are down. There's only one person who loves it when we're down, sad, angry, depressed, and willingly wanting to give up that's *Satan.* He loves to see us weak and vulnerable. But don't you give him that satisfaction Chelsea! You better not!"

"I'm not trying to, I-"

I just stopped and shook my head. "Tamara, you're the strong one in the family. Not me."

"Yes, but I go through things just as much as everyone does *sometimes even more* than anyone else. I hurt just like everyone else hurt. But I figured if I'm not strong then who else *can* be?" She squeezed my hand.

"Who else can be Chelsea?" What keeps me strong is *faith...love...and hope.* We have our gifts and talents on Earth to use to help uplift us and share with the world. What are *your* spiritual gifts? Are you an encourager, a teacher, a giver, a minister, a prayer?"

"I'm an encourager-that's what I'm good at doing," I smiled.

"Use that! That's what you're meant to do. That's *how* you get your zeal back on life and in God. You use your spiritual gifts to help shape the world. Once you get your spiritual life in order, then everything else will fall into place."

"You're right!" I chuckled to myself, "Thank you, Tamara! I really needed to hear that. I don't want to give up so easily. It starts with me!"

"Yes, it does! But you'll get there! You've got people backed in your corner willing to help you always. Because we love you!"

"I love y'all too!"

155

CHAPTER 12

One year later

London is keeping me on my toes. I spend most of my time working at Paul's shop. Sometimes I have to go out and deliver some tea packages to different locations. I find myself driving through the heart of the city or on the outskirts of the country. Paul would let me use his vehicle to run errands or to just get a feel of the life of London. I liked London a lot! London was different for me. It was so easy for me just to blend in, but once I started talking, it was all over. I pretty much have toured all the extractions there is in the city. At night, my favorite pub to visit was called Highlands. I would go there a couple of nights a week to unwind from a long day of work. I thought I would only be here for a few months, but a few months led to practically a year. It wasn't in the plan. I wanted Chelsea to respond to my letter, but she didn't. I wanted some hint that she still loved me. I guessed she forgave me but wasn't ready to love again.

Chelsea...

You're the reason why I'm still here.

I just couldn't bear to come home knowing you're not with me...knowing the only thing I have is friendship. I thought I could accept that, but staying away is teaching me how to. If the only thing to gain is friendship from the pain I caused you, I humbly accept. I was thinking aloud to myself. My thoughts were interrupted by the doorbell ringing as a customer entered the building.

"Hello! How may I help you today?" I greeted.

"Hello, mate."

The young man was looking above at the menu. "I'll take an Ole English"

"What size?"

"A cup."

Working here for a while, I realized that the majority of customers that come in usually would like just a cup of tea even though there are different sizes. I went to the tea machine and poured the young man some tea into the cup. I placed it on a saucer and added two short-bread cookies on the house for him. We serve many pastries at the shop; the shortbread is complimentary. Kids can also get one free cookie when asked. I was the only one up front while Paul and another associate by the name of Gregory were in the back prepping the food. Gregory is fairly new. He started a few months after I did. He was a bit on the quiet side. He was never neat and also looked as if he needed a pair of new clothes. When I try to make conversation, he usually nods or comes off short. He had dark hair and eyes. He was just a tad bit shorter than me. He looks to be a couple of years older than me. Or life hit him hard, and he's a couple of years younger. It wasn't only that way with me, but with the rest of the staff as well. Paul usually has him in the back prepping the food, or washing the dishes. Sometimes, after Paul would talk to him, he would later reply to me, "What a strange sort," I would nod because he is strange indeed. Abby is another associate who works at the shop. Abby is the youngest worker here. She is very friendly and bubbly. I feel like she the exact replica of a younger Kyla. Abby floats around just like me. We go to each station and help out when needed. She was off for the day, so I was the only one working the front. I love working the front. I can speak and mingle with the customers. I can also make extra tips. The only extra thing that I would have to do is make sure to clean the tables and seats every hour.

The shop wasn't that big, so it wasn't too much to clean-only when it gets super busy. Today wasn't so busy. I've only had one customer so far, just waiting for the brunch rush. So far, our regulars haven't made it in just yet. But their coming. The doorbell rang as our first regular walked in.

"Hello! How may I help you today?"

Nothing

The man walked to the booth, took off his hat, and sat down. He comes every day at the same time. Sometimes even twice a day. He normally doesn't say anything except what he wants to order, which is the same thing every single day. He was a tall, older gentleman. He puts me in the mind of Gregory-just taller. He carries himself like a beggar on the streets, the look of someone homeless. He always has his dog with him, but leaves the dog outside tied to a post. The dog looked to be an old black Labrador. The dog was friendly and playful. When I cleaned the tables outside, he allowed me to pet him. I would give him a few scrapes of bacon. I wished some of that niceness from the dog would rub off on the owner. I turned around and got the cup of tea ready. He liked the honey chi tea with a grain muffin to eat. He also makes sure that I don't forget his shortbreads either. Sometimes, I can't help but laugh at the people I encounter here.

"Here you go." I placed his order on the table.

He lifted his finger to count the cookies. "Thank you." he whispered.

"Is there anything else you need?"

He took his cup and sipped his tea. I just looked at him. "All right then," I turned and walked back to the counter.

Yep, he surely is a strange one, I thought to myself. I walked back to the counter, picked up a rag, and wiped it down. I turned to the front and the man was just staring at me.

"Do you need anything else?" I asked He went back to sipping his tea.

He was the only customer so far, so I went outside to catch some air. The gentleman's dog happily greeted me as I rubbed his fur. He licked all over my hand. I pulled out a piece of bacon from my apron and fed it to the dog. On one of the outside tables, there was a folded newspaper and a bit of trash. I picked up the newspaper to read today's daily news. The early afternoon began to rise because the traffic on the streets was quickly picking up as well as the sound. I was reading about how the city was going to create new technology to help industrialize the rapid growth of computer designs, hardware, and applications. They want to find ways to help integrate and enhance better software. I was reading when the bell of the door rang behind me. I looked at the man, and he looked at the newspaper I was reading.

"Just absolute rubbish!" he grumbled aloud. He walked to the dog and untied his leash. "Come on, Sam." He let out a deep cough as they headed down the street. As I watched them go, I thought to myself, I wonder how the many stories he could tell that are worn all over him.

I'm curious to know.

This man might hold some use of interest for me.

***

The rest of the time spent at the shop was pretty slow. We had a few customers, and I ended up having around thirty dollars' worth of tips. The night quickly approached us, and I waited as Paul made his count of day to add to his safe in the back. Gregory stopped in to tell us he was gone for the night. Paul always carried a pouch with him that contained some of the money from the store. He didn't dare to leave a lot of money in the store. The most left would be $200.00. The rest he would take home and leave to carry it to the bank the next morning. We locked up the shop and made our way back to Paul's house. On the way home, Paul was talking about what he wanted to do next in the company. He was talking about maybe expanding it so that the store can appeal more to college students. They can come there with their laptops and do their schoolwork. I agreed that it wouldn't be such a bad idea, but of course, if he expands, then he will need more staffing. Then it went back to just keeping things the way they are for the time being.

We made it home and there was an extra vehicle in the driveway.

He looks over at me and smiles. "Looks like we have company tonight."

We walked inside the house. The aroma of food filled my nose, and I was ready to dive into whatever Chloe had fixed. I was hungry.

Chloe greeted us at the door and gave her husband a kiss.

"Dinner is just about ready. Katie is upstairs in her room and Bryce is running around here somewhere." She laughed and looked at me. "Seth, I have a friend here who I would like for you to meet."

So that's why Paul smiled at me. "Ok, let me get freshen up and I will be out shortly." I turned around and walked to my bedroom.

"Ok, we will see you shortly," she said after me.

I walked into my room and closed the door. I went and flopped right on the bed. I was looking at the ceiling. I didn't want this. Not tonight. I wasn't ready for a match-up at the moment. I wasn't even thinking about any romantic interactions of any kind at all. I rubbed my face.

"I'm hungry, so I got to face her," I quietly said to myself. I breathed out deeply.

I heard a faint giggle.

It was a familiar giggle.

I got up from my bed and looked underneath.

There Bryce was hiding under my bed.

"Boo!" He laughed.

Bryce was about four years old. He was always in my room hiding from the rest of the family. He was a very active youngster. I adored playing with him though. He was the substitute for me missing my nieces and nephews back home. He crawled from under my bed.

"Hello! Would you play with me?"

"I can't today little man. Your mom is looking for you. It's about time to eat. Are you hungry?"

He nodded his head. "I am a little bit."

"Ok, well let's go downstairs and get something to eat."

I wrestled him off my bed, and we walked downstairs to the dining area. Everyone was pretty much at the table. Katie was in her seat. She was nine years old and looked exactly like Paul. She's a bit shy but carries his mannerisms. Paul was already seated, and Chloe came in placing dishes on the table. Behind her was a stunning individual. She carried a bowl of salad in her hands.

"Hello," she said to me, and she placed the salad bowl on the table.

"Hello," I responded. "I'm Seth."

I reached out my hand and she shook it. Chloe walks in with the table napkins.

"Seth, this is my friend Anna. She will be joining us tonight for dinner. Anna this is our friend Seth."

"Yes, we just met." She laughed at Chloe.

We sat down to eat. Chloe made some lasagna with breadsticks and a side salad. Anna was a pretty woman. She looks like she is mixed with some black or maybe something Spanish. She had big, round eyes and hair that hung to her shoulders. She was tall and slender.

"So, Anna, where are you from?" I asked her.

"I'm originally from Portugal. My family moved here when I was eight. I recently left here and went back home to Portugal. I'm here visiting my family and friends."

"Do you think you will ever move back to London?"

"I haven't decided just yet. I may consider it later down the line." She took a bite of her salad. "Chloe said that you are from

America. That's one place I would love to see! What brought you here to London?"

"My dad. Before he passed away, he always wanted to travel to Europe and visit the beautiful countries here. So, I decided to fulfill his dreams as well as my own. I'm a journalist and editor as well. So, visiting these beautiful countries helps me to write amazing stories."

"That's very riveting Seth! I would hope to read one of your stories one day. Will you be living in London permanently?"

"I don't know. I've been here just a little over a year. I haven't decided just yet."

Paul and Chloe smiled at each other. We ate the rest of our dinner. The food and the conversation with Anna were very satisfying. She was a very delightful and sweet person. I was sitting there listening to her, but Chelsea captivated my very thoughts. I started to think and wonder what she was doing at this very moment.

Is she thinking about me?

Or does she miss me like I miss her?

I haven't heard anything from her in over a year. Was I just fooling myself? Was I stuck in this sentimental bubble of hope for Chelsea? Or is this God's way of showing me to move on and give Anna a chance?

I was interrupted by my thoughts when Chloe asked if I would like to have some pie for dessert. I declined the offer. I couldn't put anything else in my stomach at the moment. Anna declined the offer as well.

"I should be heading home now." Anna walked to the chair to put on her jacket. "It was nice meeting you, Seth. Maybe we can grab some coffee one day, and you can tell me all about America."

"Sure! I would like that."

Chloe led Anna outside. Paul looked at me.

"Well, what do you think? She's pretty and seems really interested in seeing you again."

"Yes, she does. But I'm just not ready for that right now."

Paul looked at me. "Is she why you're still here?"

"Yeah." I turned around and walked to my room.

***

Paul gave me the day off today. He said that he had more than enough staff to cover all shifts and since I've been working for him, I've never had a workday off. I didn't mind not having a workday off, it actually kept my mind proactively not thinking of home and what's there. I didn't argue about having a day off. I wanted to enjoy the moment and get back to writing in my journal. I haven't written in my journal in a long time, and I felt completely empty and off balance with my train of thoughts. I had forgotten what I had previously written before. This was so unusual for me, and I didn't want this to continue again. Not writing for a long time seems like I have to recreate my stories all over again. My format doesn't seem authentic to me anymore. I have to get out of this stance and bring back my energy of writing. Paul let me keep his car and I went to a park that was located by a river. It was actually within the area of the shop. I sat on a bench that was located in the park. I looked around to absorb everything that was around the area. I just took it all in. I sat there to meditate on my thoughts.

After a moment, I pulled out my journal and let my pencil do the work. I figured once I get settled on where I'm actually going to be living then I will write my book. I don't know if I want to go back to the States. Part of me wants to escape and keep going. But if I keep going, will there be happiness waiting for me at the end? Then the other part of me...misses that element of home.

Woof! Woof!

I looked up and saw Sam running up toward me.

"Hey, boy!" I got off the bench and rubbed his head. "Are you having fun in the park?"

Sam started licking my face and jumping up on me. "I don't have any bacon on me today."

"Sam?!"

I turned around and there was the grumpy man heading straight toward us.

"Sam!" he stopped and bent over. Cough! Cough! Sam?!" He started hooking the leash on Sam's collar. "I've told you about running up to people!"

"He didn't bother me at all! You have a friendly dog!" I was making conversation, but he wasn't looking in my direction. "I see you guys at the tea shop all the time."

He hooks the lease to his collar. He paused once he saw my journal on the bench. I looked at him and then at my journal.

"I'm Seth Calloway! I'm a journalist and editor! I write stories."

"Humph," he snorted. "There are no real stories anymore, only rubbish. A true writer writes without extracting the details."

"I would like to hear your story sir." I urged in his response.

"Come on, Sam" He walks away and started coughing.

I watched them go.

I wondered if maybe he was a writer himself, and something happened to his business. Or maybe he wanted to be a writer, but his path led him to do something else. Maybe it was a regret of some kind. I don't know, but I'm curious to find out. A man who completely lives his life on the streets of London must have a story behind this. I went back to writing in my journal.

***

Days had gone by, and I hadn't seen the grumpy old man or Sam in a while. When I had any extra free time, I would walk around the streets to see if I could spot him somewhere. Maybe he chose a new spot to hang out. I just hoped that nothing was seriously wrong with him. He had a bad cough the last time that I saw him. The shop was pretty steady even though it was raining outside. Anna came in to get a drink of tea. I sat down to talk to her for a bit. She had taken a job at the university in bi-lingual studies to help those who want to learn another language. She was leaving in a few days to go back to Portugal to bring back some of her items. Even though nothing can come out of our interaction...I enjoyed talking to her again.

CHAPTER 13

Today was beautiful. The Sunday afternoon was pleasant, and I felt a bit like relaxing today. I've hardly ever worked on a Sunday. If I do, it will be just revising a column that I did or someone else's. I decided to go to the park and spend the day writing for a bit. I was walking around the park, trying to find a spot, when I noticed some feet away the tall grumpy man. His back was facing toward me, and there was Sam lying beside his feet. It was a bit hot today, so maybe the heat is draining him. From the back of him, it seems as though he was resting in the sun. I walk toward them. I know Sam was exhausted from the heat. He didn't raise his head or run up toward me. I did kneel down to rub his head. I sat right beside the old man. He was indeed asleep.

"Haven't your father ever told you not to disturb someone while they sleep?" he said to me.

Or so I *thought* he was asleep.

"Yeah, but that was before he passed away. Now I'm limited on what he can tell me."

The old man raised one of his eyes and looked at me.

"Oh, well I'm sorry to hear that."

"Thanks."

A moment's pause.

"So, it's pretty hot today. Are you from around here?" I asked.

He blinked both of his eyes.

"I'm from everywhere"

"I'm from America. I live in the state of Georgia. I'm here traveling and exploring the many countries here." He had a smile on his face.

"Why are you here, Mr. Calloway?"

I was shocked that he remembered my name. "I told you-I'm here exploring."

He turned his head and looked directly at me.

"No, you're not. You're here escaping...from pain, love, loss, poverty. When people leave, they leave because of something that they're going through...sometimes not even because they *want* to leave."

"Is that what happened to you?"

"I was born in London, but my great-grandparents were immigrants from Ireland. My great-great-grandfather married a Jewish homemaker. So, I'm part Irish and Jewish. Around those times were the Great Famine and the persecution of the Jews. It was hard times for my ancestors."

"That's why they came here. For a better life-"

"*Better?!*" he retorted. "My great-great-grandfather had poured his sweat, blood, and tears into making the London Underground. Working just like an immigrant whose wages are free upon the territory of men whose country is theirs. My dad helped build the bridge. He also worked for the printing press just to earn a little more money. You see that church over there-"

He pointed to church which the peak of its point stood out in the very far distance.

"That's where we gathered to worship and pray and to beg for food. During those times lad, immigrants suffered. Many passed away from poverty, illnesses, malnutrition, and crime. And *Ella?!*" He started coughing again.

Who is Ella? I thought to myself.

I reached out my arms to help him, but he jerked away from me.

"I'm fine." he mumbled.

"You know this world has a lot of history...a lot good and a lot bad. Over time, history has changed for the better, let me say *improved* for the most part. Technology has created a wave in this era to make things a little better than before." He shook his head.

"No! No! No!" he shouted as he pounded his leg, "You don't get it! That's why I say the news is rubbish; it negates the real information. History isn't meant to change, Mr. Calloway; it's meant to teach and to provide us wisdom to create a *better* history!"

"Yes! But change is needed to make a better history!" I argued.

The older man got up from the bench.

"Look around you. Have things *really* changed? *Has the world really changed for you Seth and your culture?*" He was looking deep into *my* very own soul I felt, "We can build, engineer, destroy, program anything or everything that exists on this planet today...but we have to create a better person within-it's the *people* who have to change. *That's why history repeats itself!* Because if people don't change, nothing will. Look at *my people.*" He walks away with Sam lagging behind him.

"Hey, what's your name?" I shouted after him.

He stopped and turned to face me.

"Elijah."

He walks away.

He is right, I thought to myself. Their way of life has improved from where it used to be, but history is still the same, from his culture and definitely from mine. There's still so much inequality, racism, and persecution for those who are different from one another. It's hinted around here and there above the surface, but it's deeply rooted underneath. He's not a grumpy old man. He's a man that's entangled with scars deeply rooted from the grave of his ancestors. Deeply rooted in the ongoing suppression of his culture.

I understood him now.

His grumpiness and anger were only merely to the fact that nothing has changed with the treatment of his people. History hasn't changed because people haven't changed. Life still aches because we're still reminded of history by the things that we go still through on a regular basis.

Just like my people, we're constantly reminded that we're black even when we think things are getting better. The difference between me and Elijah is I can't go through life being anger and bitter about it. Because when things do go bad, God does show up and show out. Life is still beautiful beyond its adversaries. Good always triumphs over bad. There are still a lot of good people in this world-with some it just *takes* a moment to see. For others, it's unseen.

I sat on the bench and watched the glow of the sun. I sat there and just closed my eyes.

I felt the sun's rays glisten on my cheeks.

Even though it was hot, the rays of the sun felt different. I felt the urge to laugh, and I did!

I smiled at God's light. And He smiled back at me.

***

The next day at work, Elijah came in wanting the usual that he gets every time he comes in. He had on a new sweater that was worn above his regular shirt. Sam was tied to the same pole outside. I went outside to give him some scraps of bacon. I cleaned the tables outside and walked back in. Elijah was still sipping on his tea. Abby was working today, so she was waiting on the few customers at the counter. I went up behind the counter to help get the customer's orders out of the way. Once they were gone, I walked up to Elijah and sat down another cup of coffee.

"I didn't order another cup of coffee!" Elijah said.

"It's on the house," I said, and I sat down right in front of him.

"Thank you but you didn't have to do that. I was perfectly fine."

"Hey, you looked like you needed another cup; like I said, it's on the house. We reward our long-term customers here."

"I've been coming here for over ten years, and I've never been rewarded before," he argued.

"Well, I've started a new trend."

"Good trend," he muttered sipping his new cup of tea.

"Why are you always so grumpy?" I asked him. "Under that coat of armor, you seem like a nice guy."

"Grumpy?!" he snarled as if he were the happiest person on the planet. "I'm not grumpy, I'm just-"

"Who's Ella?" I interjected.

He started coughing. "Ella?"

"Yes, you mentioned her name in conversation with me yesterday. Is she your wife?"

"*Ella,*" he whispered to himself. He rubbed his head between his hands.

"You, okay?" I asked. "We don't have to talk about Ella if you don't want to."

"You asked why I was grumpy. Well, I don't mean to be." He reached to take a sip of his tea, and his hand was shaken as he lowered the cup to the saucer. I saw the water glisten in his eyes. "Ella was my sister...my twin sister. She passed away when I was nine years old. You remember when I said that times were really dark then?"

I nodded my head.

"They were dark. People were angry, and crime was very high." He looked over my shoulder as if he was drifting back in time. "I had a high fever that day, and Mother made me stay at home. Ella begged and begged my mother to go to school. She was going to be in a stage play, so she wanted to go to the rehearsal. She was quite a performer-very shy though. Very shy. We always walk back and forth to school together. But she didn't make it back home that day." He shook his head. "She didn't make it home." Tears streamed down his face.

"I remember the sound of the knock that day when they came to tell my dad the news. They found her lying against the bank, beaten and raped...some of her bones broken." He whimpered out a breath, "My sister, my best friend...never to perform again."

"I'm sorry Elijah," I replied. He was still grieving the loss of his sister. "Did they ever find the person who did it?"

"No, they never did find *them.*" He looked at me. "Now you know why I'm so angry."

He got up from his seat and walked outside.

Wow, this man has gone through so much, I thought. *He lost his sister at such a young age and has never gotten beyond that point of healing. Not only is she his sister but his twin-the closest bond there is on this planet.* My pain ached with his. He lost his sister years ago and I lost both of my parents. I *have* to help this man. I went to Paul to ask if I could come back in a couple of hours. He nodded to me. He probably heard the conversation from behind the booth. I ran outside to catch up to Elijah. I spotted him walking around the corner with Sam. I ran up faster to meet him.

"Hey Elijah, where are you heading to?" I asked.

"The usual!" he replied.

"How about I put you up in a hotel for the night?" He stopped and turned to face me.

"Look, Mr. Calloway, I will be just fine by myself heading that way." He pointed down the street.

"But I won't," I said. "Besides, they say it's supposed to get really cold tonight. How about a nice, warm spot to rest your head?"

He just looked at me.

"Come on, I will feel much better knowing you were out the cold."

I put my arm over his shoulder and guided him to a nice hotel that was in the area. Instead of me paying for the night, I paid for a week. I wanted him to get some rest. He'd been coughing a lot, and it hadn't gotten any better. He reminded me of how my dad was before he died. Now he has a place to stay for the time being. He could take a nice shower and eat hot meals. I provided him with a nice pair of clothes, a blanket, and some medicine. I also brought him and Sam food to eat for the week. I made sure that I stopped by to see him every day. One day I stopped by a toy shop and bought a game of checkers and went to Elijah's room to play.

"I haven't played checkers in a long time, since I was nine," Elijah said.

"Well, it's still the same way. I'll let you win if I have to." I laughed.

"Oh no, we play for real. My dad never let me just win."

"Really?! My dad too! I always played games with my dad, or we watched games together." I took the game out of the box and began the set-up.

"Yep, we were close! He died of cancer about a couple of years ago. My mother died when I was young as well. They were the best parents ever. I miss them so much." I was beginning to feel my emotions creep up.

"I'm sorry for your loss also."

"You know what my dad used to always tell me and my siblings?"

He shook his head.

"He always said that God sends us rain to appreciate the sunshine."

There was silence for a brief moment as we were playing.

"Your sister and my parents are resting now. We have to keep living. God is still using us to do more in this world, that's why we are still here. You have to find your inner peace, Elijah. By being angry and bitter, you'll be just like *them*. Your sister wouldn't have wanted that."

He wiped his eye with his hand. Then he jumped twice over my red tokens.

"No, she wouldn't. I went homeless because I wanted to be alone and I was just completely angry with myself, God, and everyone. I thought why *her?* Why *me?* After I turned homeless, there was no turning back. Sometimes I thought I was just better off." He chuckled to himself. "But look how that turned out?"

"It's never too late. Every day can be a better tomorrow. In order to heal from pain, you must let things go."

"How?"

"Forgive and let go...then play checkers!" He chuckled to himself.

After that, our bond grew closer. Elijah was laughing and smiling more. He was eager to tell me stories of his life and family. He was also eager to listen to my stories. Even though he wasn't completely off the streets, he had a better approach to fixing himself up. Paul, Chloe and the kids had gotten attached to him as well. Chloe would invite him over to have supper with us. He will eat and tell the kids stories. Sometimes he would even stay the night. I would give him my bed as I slept on the sofa. When the mornings come, he will eat and leave but somehow make his way back to the shop. Paul paid him to help out at the shop. He will clean and make sure to stock the supplies every day. He didn't get paid much but it was something. He seemed happy. And I was happy for him. But a small part of me still missed home.

CHAPTER 14

I was super tired. It was extremely busy or at least it felt like it because Paul and I were like the *only* workers there. Abby was scheduled off today, but when we asked if she could come in to help cover a shift, she had prior engagements. Gregory just didn't bother showing up period.

Lately, he has been standoffish and not saying anything hardly to anyone this past couple of weeks. Well, that was pretty much his normal, anyway. Elijah would have definitely been thrown in as a cook today or prepping the drinks. He didn't show up today at all... a matter of fact, for the last couple of days, I haven't seen him. I hope everything was ok with him. Once the last customer left, and Paul locked the doors, I flopped down in a chair.

"I just want to go home and go straight to bed," I said. "Take a shower, then hit the sack. I don't even want the covers over me."

"Sack mate?!" Paul asked.

I laughed, "Yes, that American slang for bed."

"I just want to go to a pub and drink all night."

He sprawled down right beside me. "Any other time I would be right there with you bro, but today *I'm tired*!"

Paul laughed and put the money into a zip bag. "You know, I think you just might be right, mate."

He got off the counter and checked the locks to make sure they were securely locked.

"This will be one of the largest deposits I'll make tomorrow at the bank in a long time. We made close to $6k and *that's* without tips."

"Well, it sure *felt* like we did that much," as I stretched and yawned, "You sure it wasn't more?"

"Maybe tomorrow will be the same profit if no one shows up like today."

We were heading to the back to turn off the alarm. Everything was turned off, from the machines to the lights. Every station was completely stocked with materials, and everything was put away.

When we stepped outside, the night air was cool and quiet. It seems a little weird because usually when we close for the night, the streets are still busy, and people are walking on the sidewalks.

But today it was not busy at all. Sort of like a calm, silent night. Mr. Tabor, who owns the next-door cake shop, the car was still in the parking lot. He must have been just as busy as we were.

Another thing that's odd is the parking lot is usually filled with a dozen cars, but today, there are only five. Two of the cars were parked, I'd never seen in the parking lot before. It was just a strange night.

"It's a little nippy tonight. I hope Elijah will be all right tonight."

"Yeah, wherever he is," I hopped into the car and fastened up. "I hope he found somewhere to nestle in and keep warm."

"He might come by the house later," Paul said.

"Maybe," I said to him. Elijah had done that a few times when we hadn't seen him all day; he showed up at the door, knocked, and we would let him in. If the kids were still up, he would bring them to the living room to read a book or sometimes tell his own stories. We pulled off quietly into the night.

Paul cut on the radio to his local station, and we listened to some music on the drive.

He turned toward me. "So, Chloe and I were thinking about taking a family trip for the weekend next month; I wanted to ask you if you could watch the shop for us. Unless you want to come with us, we wouldn't mind, mate."

I sat there thinking, should I take another trip somewhere that I've never been to? I would love to go to Africa, the motherland. But a trip like that I wouldn't want to go by myself. I would love to bring a wife.

"We have some family in Germany that we haven't seen in a while. So, we decided to go plan a short trip to see them."

"That sounds like fun. But I want you guys to enjoy your family time. I've been under your wing for a while now, so I'll be happy to watch the shop for you."

Paul and his family were great company. They helped me through this journey in a lot of ways. I was beyond in their debt. They provided me with room, board, transportation, and salary. When I think about the many good people in this world, they are at the top of my list for real. They are of European descent and have treated me like family like I'm one of their own. They have shown nothing but kindness and hospitality to me since the first time I met them.

"Thanks, mate. I appreciate it."

"Anytime man."

The low heat was warming up the vehicle from the cool night quickly. I was beginning to get a little bit hot. I was exhausted. I was ready to go to bed, but the heat now is keeping me up and alert. Paul took the quicker route home which was one of the back roads along the bank of the river. It seemed like we were the only people on the road. When we made it to a traffic light to stop, I reached out my hand to turn the heat down a bit.

"Thanks, I was beginning to get hot myself. You know this is strange for it to be a cold night like this one."

I looked at him as his eyes got bigger and his face fell completely white like a ghost. I turned my head toward the direction he was looking- *Bam!!*

The force of the hit lifted the car off the ground and flipped us in the air.

Bang!

Flip

Bang!

Flip

Bang!

Flip

Bang!

My head struck the dashboard, and the crunch of metal and the shatter of glass echoed. Pain shot throughout my whole entire body. I felt like the rest of my body was broken into pieces.

Blood trickled down my nose and face. I didn't know if I hit my nose, head, or what! I knew I was upside down. My head was beginning to feel weightless, and I felt like couldn't breathe. I was trying to call out for help, but I my mouth felt numb. I felt like no sound was coming out no matter how hard I tried. Or at least maybe I lost my hearing. The airbag was flat against my nose. My heart was beating rapidly and my chest was burning.

"*Help,*" I whispered.

I couldn't see Paul!

"Paul" I whispered. I tried to use my strength to call out for help. I felt like I still couldn't hear myself. Then I heard voices coming near.

"*Hurry up! We have to hurry before the cops show up*"

"*Just help me find the money pouch!*" I heard a familiar voice.

"*Do you think that they are still alive?*"

"*Who cares?! Just help me find the money!*"

"*My truck took a real good beating. Good thing it only cost us $300 bucks.*"

"*I see it!!!*"

I heard scrambling noises from the back of me.

"Gre-!" I tried to yell his name above my whisper.

"Help Greg!"

"*Hey, I think one of them just called your name!*"

"*Shit! We got to get out of here!*"

"*Hurry mate!*"

"*Got it!*"

"*We got to get rid of them now!*"

"*What?!*"

"*Look, I'm not going through all of this just to get sent to prison!*"

"*Okay, I don't know about this! What are you going to do?!*"

Greg's voice sounded nervous.

"We are getting back in the truck! Let's move!"

"Help!" I cried out.

My body ached all over. I didn't hear any voices anymore.

I felt my body tremble all over.

Please don't go into shock.

"Paul!" I couldn't hear anything from my left side, even a hint of whimper. I have to find Paul, make sure that he's okay. I have to get out of here. I started to move my arms to push myself up from the side door that was still attached. I suddenly hear the sound of a motor and a squeal of tires. The motor roars closer and closer and closer and clo-

Wham

My back jolted upward. I felt the car moving fast. *Oh no!* I have to get out of here. I tried to move my hand to unfasten the seat belt. Then suddenly the car flipped.

Bang! Flip!

Bang! Flip!

Bang! Flip!

Splash! Flip!

Splash! Flip!

Splash!

Silence

Darkness covered my eyes...

***

Awoke!

I inhaled a cool weep of breath and opened my eyes.

My head rested on the airbag. I started trembling again. I felt the cold rush of water coming up against my legs faster and faster up. I lifted up my head and pushed the airbag out of the way as fast as I could to look over my shoulder.

"Oh no!" Paul wasn't there! I looked around and I didn't see him anywhere in the car. I quickly reached to unfasten my belt. The belt was jammed against the door, and I couldn't feel the base of the belt at all. The water was now upon my upper waist.

"Umph," I grunted loudly as I tried to pull the seatbelt. The seat was jammed tightly against my waist. "Come on! Come On!" I pulled as hard as I could to yank the seatbelt from the base. I was fighting against the pain in my body, fighting against the cold water that continued to rise, fighting against seeing death if I didn't get out. I had to steady my breath because the temperature of the water seemed colder and colder. I tried to pull the belt again. I felt the belt dig deep against the skin. I didn't care about the pain or what it was doing. I keep pulling and pulling. The water was getting above my shoulders.

"Please God help me!" I pulled again. "*Urgh!!!!!!!!!*"

It didn't budge at all. I was trying to think quickly about what else I could do or use. The car was sinking, and I was glued to it. No one was around to help me.

Chelsea!

I would never get a chance to tell her how much I loved her. I will never again see her beautiful face. I would never get to hear that soft-spoken voice. I would never get a moment to explore those hidden mysteries that make her who she really is. If only I could have seen her just one last time...

The water was getting above my face. I started counting to ten, waiting for the seconds before the water would cover me completely...

I took in a deep breath as the water went above my head. I started pulling against the seatbelt again. I had to give as many tries as I could. I had to go out giving it as much as I could give. I was a fighter just like my dad. I was a fighter just like my mom. I kept pulling and pulling and pulling. My lungs felt like they were about to burst open. I felt my body jerked against the water. I had a beautiful life. I enjoyed the good and bad of it all. I had finally found love. Of course,

I've always had love...but I *finally* found my love.

Chelsea's face illuminated from under the water,

Oh, what a picture! I thought to myself.

I took it all in...

Until my last breath came out.

***

The headlights were peeking above the surface of the water. I left Sam over by Paul who lay lifeless against the grass. I ran as fast as I could, but I didn't know if I was running fast enough.

"I'm coming, Seth!! Hang on in there!" I dived into the water.

This old body hasn't swum in water for a long time. I usually go to the water whenever I haven't bathed in weeks just to freshen up or to get my joints moving. The headlights were still afloat as I swam closer.

Please God let me help him, I thought to myself as I approached the light. I took in a deep breath and went underwater. I looked around to see if I could spot Seth anywhere. I saw him still sitting in the seat of the car. I swam into the open window. I swam up to Seth and grabbed his face. I shook it.

"Seth!" I cried out under the water.

His eyes remained closed.

I looked around the seat and saw that he was still attached to his seatbelt. I pulled on it-

"Urgh!" I swallowed in a gulp of water. My throat began to burn, and I started losing oxygen.

I reached for the side of my attached belt and pulled out my knife. I cut as quickly as I could, and the belt snapped apart. I grabbed Seth and dragged him from the car. I swam back to the bank and quickly performed CPR.

CHAPTER 15

Beep

Beep

Beep

The sound vibrated in my ears. The sound was constant. I blinked my eyes. I looked around to what appeared to be a hospital room.

I'm alive!

Thank you, God!

I tried to move to shift my body and then it hit me-pain!

Then I remembered what had happened. I remember seeing a big vehicle ram into us. Then I remember hearing Gregory's voice, and another man's voice. After that came another hit, and I was completely underwater.

"Paul!"

My arm was completely bandaged. I looked on the bed to see if there was a nurse's button attached to it. The only button I saw was to adjust the bed. I pushed the button on the side of my bed to lift it up a bit. There was a knock on the door, and a nurse entered the room.

"You're awake!"

"How long had I been out?"

"A few days. You were on a ventilator the first day until your breathing was under control. On the second day, they noticed movement, but you were still unconscious." She stated looking at the monitor, "My, I must say, I'm glad to see you alive. It was a horrific thing. You and your friend were lucky."

"How is Paul doing?"

She smiled at me. "Better. He's down the hall. I am tending to him as well. He's been asking about you." She started checking my blood pressure and temperature. "He is still in a lot of pain. He has a few broken bones and a back fracture. He is pretty bang up just like you are. He was thrown from the vehicle. If the windshield glass didn't break, he wouldn't have made it."

"Did they find the men who did it?"

"No, not yet. They're looking for them." She smiled at me again.

"Well, one of them happens to be an ex-employee by the name of Gregory. I heard him talking about getting the money."

"All this for money?! That's so barbaric! I'm sure the police will be here later today or tomorrow to take your statement. What is your pain level?"

"Is twenty on the scale?"

She laughed. "I will bring some pain medication to help with that and a hot bowl of soup. How does that sound to you?"

"It sounds great."

"You've had a couple of broken ribs, and your lungs are inflamed. But you will be all right. I filled your water bottle, so try to drink plenty of water and get plenty of rest."

"Do you know who saved us?"

"I don't know his name yet. He's an older gentleman. It's such a pity; he saved your lives but injured his in the process. He has a lung infection which caused a severe case of pneumonia. It's no telling how long he's been suffering from it. Apparently, the water may have ruptured it. He's on a ventilator as we speak. He's doing ok."

I nodded.

"Do you need anything at the moment?"

"No thank you," I replied.

"Ok, I will be back shortly with some pain medication and food."

She left, and I looked back at the window. Tears streamed from my eyes. My heart poured out for this man who was willing to save me. I closed my eyes and silently prayed for the man and his family. Whoever this man is, I hope beyond hope that he gets well.

***

Chloe was sleeping in the recliner as I opened the door to Paul's room. I had a little limp from the crash, but the doctors assured me that it was only temporary. He wanted me to get up and start walking from time to time to help work the muscles in my leg.

Paul was looking up at the TV watching some crime show.

"Oy, I didn't hear you come in mate!" He had a big smile on his face. "How are you feeling?"

Chloe woke up at the sound of her husband's cheerful voice. She quickly walked up to me and gave me a hug. She looked at me and tears filled her eyes.

"We're so glad you're fine," she said. "When I checked on you, you were always resting. I didn't want to disturb you just yet."

"Yes, I got tired of lying in the bed. I had to get out. I'm just still really sore."

"Have they released you yet?"

I shook my head. "Probably within a day or two they will. How are you feeling?"

"I could be better. But I'm as good as I can get considering. I'm glad you're fine. This was no way I would have expected-"

I lifted my hand, "Hey, things can happen anywhere and anytime. We have no control over that." I moved closer to his bed. "So, you've been spending some time watching crime shows?"

"There's hardly anything on. I'm getting so bored."

I laughed. "Have you tried moving around?"

"Yes, when I have to go to the bathroom. Chloe has to help me though. There's still a lot of pain in my lower back. I will have to go to physical therapy once I get out."

"What about the shop?" I asked.

"Well, it will be closed for a couple of weeks, but I have my brother and two of my uncles that will help out. Chloe is going to help them when needed. Of course, when you're ready to go back, you can you know."

I nodded. "I told the police one of the guys was Gregory."

"Yeah, after they talked with you, they came to see me as well. Strange that he would rob me only for a small pocket of change. He was a strange one, that one. I should have had more of a guard on him."

"You didn't know as well as I didn't. I'm just thankful to God that we survived."

"Amen to that."

"Well, I'm about to head out. I'm going to go see the guy who saved our lives. They say that he's in the hospital as well but not doing so well."

"Would you thank him for me?"

I nodded. "Sure. You get some rest ok. Try to move when you can."

Paul laughed.

"He will," Chloe said. "I will make sure that he does."

"I will stop by when they release me."

I left their room and headed down to the second floor to room 2016. Nurse Joy gave me his information yesterday. I told her how much I wanted to go and thank him for what he did for me and my friend. The last update that she gave me was still the same.

They have yet taken him off the ventilator yet. I was eager to see him. I was a little afraid because I didn't know what to expect when I walked into his room.

Would his family be upset that he helped me?

Surely not!

But will they allow me to visit him?

I didn't have the answers just yet. The ring from the elevator opened the door and I was on the floor. It was the ICU area of the hospital. I went up to the nurse's station so that they could point me in the right direction. A nurse actually got up and said that she would walk me to where he was resting. She walked me to his area and my knees buckled at the sight of him. My gasp was held within. I stood there in shock and disbelief.

"Are you okay?" the nurse asked me.

"I know him," I whispered to her.

I slowly walked to his bed. His thin body was even thinner and frail. "Excuse me; do you know where they placed his dog?"

"I would check the police station. It may be there or at a nearby animal shelter." The nurse smiled and walked away.

I turned my face back at Elijah. "Oh- man!" I choked out. "Not you Elijah!"

I looked at the heart monitor, which showed a pulse beeping. There were so many tubes going inside his body. The ventilator was also connected to his body. He just looked as if he was in a peaceful sleep. I leaned over to his ear.

"Thank you, Elijah, for saving our lives. Now I want you to fight all right; you come back to us."

I smooth out his hair. Then I walked over to a chair and sat there for a while. I didn't want him to be alone.

***

The shop was a little steady today. Paul was at home doing his physical therapy. He was due to come back to work in a couple of weeks. Uncle Jake and Sy were still helping out with the shop. Abby and I were working the front of the store. When I was released from the hospital, I went to the police station to see where Sam was at. They gave me the name of the animal shelter where they normally store dogs if they belonged to someone else. Sam was so happy to see me when I checked him out. I usually bring him with me to work because no one could watch him around the clock like that. Today, he was at home with Paul and the family.

The police also informed me that they apprehended Gregory and his accomplice Clive Slater. They have been brought on charges of robbery, battery, and attempted murder. It still baffles my mind that Gregory would want to do something like that. I couldn't help but shake my head. Well, he will spend the rest of his life in prison thinking about the bad choice that he made.

I feel like the whole community knew what had happened. We are way busier now than we were before the incident happened. I don't mind it though. I'm just glad to be back to work. It helps keep my mind from thinking about my friend Elijah. I visit Elijah every day at the hospital. He has a severe respiratory failure. He's been taken off the ventilator and is now breathing on his own. He's no longer in ICU but is now in a room. He hasn't woken just yet. As soon as my shift is over, I'm heading to see him. Due to the recent incident, Paul no longer closes the shop late anymore, seven is closing time.

Today was such a beautiful day. It's been raining the past four days, so I was thankful for the sunshine. I made my way up the elevator of the hospital to Elijah's room. When I opened the door, Elijah turned his head to face me. The nurse was standing there filling something out on her chart.

"He woke up a few hours ago. He's been waiting to see you." She turned to Elijah. "Ok, Mr. Lewis I will check vitals in a few minutes."

"Yes," he whispered.

The nurse left the room. I went over to pull a chair right in front of him. He was smiling at me. "So how are you feeling?"

"I'm okay." He whispered. "How is Sam?"

I laughed. "Being Sam, he's at home with Paul." I looked at him and grabbed his hand. "Thank you, Elijah. I wouldn't be here if it wasn't for you. It breaks my heart to see you like this. I'm so sorry." Tears streamed down my face.

"Oy, Mr. Calloway," he squeezed my hand. "You saved my life too. You help me to see that there are good people worth saving. I never believed that after Ella passed, but now I do. And it's all because of you son. You helped me and don't you ever forget that."

"I'm glad I met you, Elijah; you truly are amazing."

"You are too, son; I hope she realizes it too."

"She?!"

"The person that you escaped from, the person you love-the person who you are writing about in your journal."

"Her name is Chelsea."

"I'm sure she's as beautiful as her name."

"She is. She's beautiful, loving, and blind. She makes the most beautiful paintings!" I was about to say more but I stopped myself. "I just don't know if she feels the same way about me, the way I feel about her."

"You will never know unless you go back to her. Sometimes love is not always what we expect it to be. Whom we think it should be. It's not always when we want it to be. But how will you know by staying here? Love comes in many directions, Mr. Calloway; you just have to stop running. Otherwise, you'll be just like me."

"Yeah, and what's that?" I asked him.

"Grumpy and alone."

I smiled at him. "I'm going to write about you in my book."

"I know you are. You're a writer-that's what you are! I want you to use your gift and share it with the world. I want you to touch people the way that you touched me." His eyes began to water, and he tried to lift his head to me, "You keep touching people, son, that's your gift."

I was fighting against the tears that were forming in my eyes, "Well if I decide to go back. I want you to come visit me. I will pay your fare for everything, so you don't have to worry about any expenses. I just want to see you again."

He smiles at me, "How about I'll wait to see you on the other side."

I stayed with Elijah for the rest of the day. I didn't even go home. I spent the night at the hospital. We talked and shared a lot of laughs. I didn't want to leave him that night... it was a cold night.

***

Elijah passed away at 3:42 the next morning.

God took him and laid him to rest. I was deeply saddened by the loss of my dear friend, my heart was truly broken. Not only am I going to miss my dear friend, but I'm also going to miss the one person who reminded me so much of my dad. They both always had such amazing stories and advice to share with me. They both truly had lost someone that was very special to them. Elijah will truly be missed. I went to the church that Elijah showed me before and spoke with the pastor there. He remembered Elijah and his family frequently visited the church. He showed me where the rest of his family was buried. I paid to have Elijah buried right beside his twin sister Ella. I also brought flowers to put on her tombstone. I smiled and thought to myself,

You always hear the same expression that people are placed in your life for a season, no one has ever thought, why not angels? Just as God can send people into our lives, He sends angels as well.

***

I haven't been back to work since Elijah passed. I was at home, cleaning up my room. Chloe and the kids went to her mother's house to check on her parents. Paul just finished with his section of physical therapy. He's gotten along pretty well with his exercises. He no longer walks with a cane. I'm glad he's back to almost his normal self. Or should I say that this may be his new normal that he has to adjust to? He was in the kitchen getting ready to fix him something to eat when I walked in.

"Oy, do you want some eggs and honey toast? I didn't get a chance to eat any breakfast today."

"No, I'm fine man," I paused to look at him. Life was pretty much like a blur after the incident, but it began to finally come clear after Elijah's passing. "In fact, um...Friday, I'll be heading back home."

He looked up at me from his plate, "I figured that was coming sooner or later. It seemed like there were a lot of noises coming from your room-like packing here recently."

I laughed. "Yeah, I'm going to miss you guys. It's emotional, but I'm ready for the next chapter."

"I hope she makes you happy! Of course, we'll be flying in once you get settled. I hope there's enough room."

"Of course, I have plenty of empty rooms. I can't wait for you all to see my life in the States. I um...I got something for you." I handed him an envelope of cash. "I know the incident set you back some. I wanted to thank you guys for all that you've done for me. You are truly a blessing from God."

"We can't take this mate."

"I want you to. This is practically the tips and wages I've earned since I started working for you. I want to help get you on your feet, just like you help me."

"Not only have I met a friend, you're like a brother to me. I thought my business was going to sink, but you helped me out immensely. You've been an angel mate, and we will be forever grateful." He gave me a hug. "What are you going to do with Sam?"

"I figured he'll stay here with you guys, the kids can keep him company."

"The kids have high allergies to pets that's why we never got one. I think it's best if you keep him. I'm sure Elijah would have wanted that. Sam loves you-you know."

"Thanks, man" I hugged him again.

I spent as much time as I could with the family and at the shop. It seemed like the days flew by. Friday had approached and I was on the next plane out.

Goodbye, London! Hello home!

CHAPTER 16

Miguel

"Ms. Davis, do you want us to paint the parrot blue?"

"No Sarah, you can paint the bird any color you choose. Remember this is your freestyle portrait, so you can use whatever colors you like to paint the portrait-use your imagination."

"I'm going to paint my parrot blue," said Austin.

"I am painting my parrot red with orange feathers," Miracle said.

"I'm going to put polka dots on mines," said Elizabeth.

"Polka dots?!" Ryan shrieked, "You don't know what polka dots look like!"

"Yes, I do!" Elizabeth responded, "Besides, Ms. Davis said we can paint our bird however we like."

"Is that true Ms. Davis?" Ryan asked, "Does she know what polka dots look like?"

"Sure, she does! It's her own interpretation of how she visualizes how her bird would look. Just like-"

"What's interpretation, Mr. Davis?"

"Interpretation means explanation. Or an understanding of one's actions. She's painting her picture the way she sees it, just like you're painting your picture how you see it. And that's the beauty of art; everyone has their own way on how they see things."

"Ok, I will make my parrot green, orange, and white" he responded.

I laughed.

"I want you all to continue working on your paintings until Mr. Weber arrives. He will be in here shortly to take you to your next class. I will leave the paintings on your desk to dry."

I addressed the class and walked around the classroom for a moment. Mr. Weber was one of the assistant teachers who helped the teachers with their classrooms and took students where they needed to go. I have two classes a day on the scheduled days that I work. I have one-morning class and one afternoon class. This was the afternoon class scheduled for today. After class, I was going to hang out with Heather. Lately, I've been out of my routine of practicing the piano because I've been super busy with the studio as well as painting.

I was lost in my train of thought, I didn't hear when Mr. Weber walked in. "Ms. Davis, are the kids ready to go?"

"Oh y-yes!" I stammered, "Sorry, I didn't hear you."

"That's ok!" he chuckled, "I will help you get things together."

"Class, quietly put the tops on the bottles of the paint and put the brushes in your cup. Mr. Weber is here to take you back to classes. Remember to leave your paintings on your desk to dry. I will hand them back to you later this week."

I heard the clattering and chattering of the kids getting the little bit of the materials back in place. Mr. Weber helped the kids as well by telling them how great their pictures were. When I felt that everything was neatly in order, Mr. Weber took the kids to their classrooms. I felt a bit thirsty, so I decided to grab a bottle of water in the cafeteria. On the way down the hallway, I heard a familiar tune hum in my ear. It was a familiar tune that I remembered when I was a little girl. I had a musical box that played The Dance of the Sugar Plum Fairy. I loved the song so much that I wanted my mom to put me in ballet classes just so I could one day dance in the Nutcracker. Of course, ballet lessons were a bit expensive, so my mom would always say "Maybe one year." Instead of heading to get a bottle of water, I turned down the hallway to the music. I knew my way around the entire blind school, so I knew the music was coming from the music room.

When I reached the room, I felt the door slightly closed, and I pushed it open to walk inside. The music was still playing from the piano. Whoever was playing this piece was extraordinarily good! I listened as the music played. It sounded a bit different from the original score, but just as good-maybe even better with the added twist. I've never heard music played so intricately as the way this person played the keys. It was beautiful. When the song was over, I applauded the musician.

"Chelsea?!" Heather pronounced, "I'm sorry if I went over our time. I wanted Miguel to finish this music sheet before I left to meet you."

"No, we have plenty of time. I heard the music while I was walking to the cafeteria. I wanted to hear the rest."

"How did you like it?" a voice that sounded like a melody in a song.

"I love it!" I responded.

"Gracious Senorita, it's not every day that my music attracts the company of a beautiful woman."

Heather and I laughed then I heard Heather's footsteps walking towards me.

"Come in and listen as we play," she said and grabbed my hand to walk me to her piano bench, then sat me right next to him, "Miguel, this is Chelsea, and Chelsea, this is Miguel."

I stretched out my hand, and I felt Heather's hand grab mine to shake his. "Nice to meet you, Miguel."

"Pleasure is all mine, Senorita."

"Chelsea, you might remember Miguel; he was attending the school right around the time you were here."

"Really?! I don't remember the name. Were you here the whole entire time?"

"No, not long. My dad got a job offer in New York, so we moved up there for a while."

"Miguel became fluent as a pianist in New York, and then he did some studies in Paris. He's reached many accolades as a pianist as well as a composer. He's come here to help assist me with music." She touched my shoulder, "I've been teaching Chelsea how to play the keys. She's becoming quite a stir around here."

"No-not me! I only play for fun that's all."

"Well, maybe we can play together sometimes," Miguel said.

"I love how you played Dance to the Sugar Plum Fairy! I used to have a music box that played that tune when I was little. My mom gave it to me one year for Christmas. I just loved it."

"We're getting ready to start early practice for our Christmas symphony event that will be coming up shortly. I hope you will be there in attendance, Chelsea."

"I hope so. I will have to see."

"I will save you a ticket. Heather, are you ready for the next number?"

"Yes, fire away!"

Miguel started playing the next piece for the symphony. I just sat there listening to every piece of the music. It was beautiful! I drifted into thinking about Seth... Where was he?

What was he doing?

Is he thinking of me as I was thinking of him?

I was thinking about the time we were in the park, and I was lying on him as he read a book to me. I didn't listen to the words of the book; I just listened only to him. The way he held my hand at The Nutcracker, the way he holds my hand all the time...as if he never wants to let me go. When I paint, I can feel him watching every stroke of my brush, and I can hear every scribble of his pen as he writes in his journal. Oddly enough, both sounds seem to just sync together. His presence was always so comforting to me. And even in such a quiet place, our spirits are interwoven into this powerful source of kinship, where love illuminates from our soul. That's how deep our connection was. I was completely in love with him...

Until now

Where love's familiar, is at an interception.

***

I am home.

There's nothing like the hustle and bustle of the streets of Atlanta. The place where nothing ever gets old, only dreams get bigger. And when you put in your days' work, then you nestle into your quiet home, or hit up a hot spot until the next morning. Zach was waiting for me when I got off the plane. I told him in advance that I would be carrying extra luggage with me. Sam was tailing right behind me as we were approaching Zach's truck. Zach was smiling from ear to ear when he saw me. I walked up to him. "What's up, bro!" I gave him a long hug and we laughed.

"Man, it's been a long time. We missed you here. I felt like nothing was the same after you left."

"A part of me felt like I really was gone long, and then the other part looks short now that I'm back home."

"Do you think you will venture out and do it again?"

"Hell yeah! I probably won't stay as long as I did this go-round because there are so many places I would love to see, man! A lot!"

"I hear ya. Maybe we can do a family trip together."

"Absolutely!"

"Who is this right here? Are you Sam?" Zach bent down and started rubbing all over Sam. Sam began to lick him. "He's very friendly."

"Yeah, he is." I started putting the bags in the car. "How are you holding up?"

"I'm doing well. Thanks for asking." I told him about Elijah and his passing over the phone before I left London. I opened the back seat and Sam jumped right in.

"Well, everything is basically the way you left it before you left. You don't have any cobwebs lying around; sis made sure she came in and dusted your entire condo."

"Thanks to sis."

"I know you're probably tired and want to go home. But on Tuesday, the family was going to go out and have some dinner. We want to celebrate your return. There's also someone who I'd like you to meet?"

"Oh! Who is she?"

"Well while you were out exploring the world, I stayed exploring home. I-uh…I'm engaged." He looked over at me.

"Oh really?!" I shook his shoulders, "Congratulations man! So proud of you! I hope she knows what she's getting herself into. It's no walk in the park in this family."

He chuckled. "Or in any family!"

"That's right!" I looked out the window. "Hey before you drop me off, I want you to take me someplace first."

"All right! Where to?"

I gave him the address to Chelsea's house. I told him that I hadn't heard from her in over a couple of years and I wanted to see if she was ok. We pulled up to the long, winding driveway to Chelsea's house.

What?! was my first thought.

Nothing.

The house was demolished. The only thing left was the base structure and some pieces of scattered wood that lay everywhere on the ground. This explains why I haven't heard anything from Chelsea. She's no longer at this residence anymore. There was a brink of pain that rippled in my body.

"They don't live here anymore," I said to myself.

"Is her number still the same?" Zach asked.

"No, it's disconnected. I tried calling her once we landed." "I'm sure you'll get in contact with her again."

"Yeah," I said convincingly.

But I wasn't that convinced. She didn't tell me anything from the previous letters that she was moving. Not even a hint. Did she

move because of me? Or did she move because something happened?

For the rest of the drive home, I was completely in my own thoughts. I was angry, hurt, and broken all at the same time. I know Zach was trying to cheer to me up by talking about the girls and his new fiancé, but I wasn't immersed in conversation. I wasn't even remotely fascinated as he talked about his new fiancé. Don't get me wrong, I am truly happy for him. I love that he's happy and that he's in a better place. I just didn't want to hear it! I didn't want to hear about love and happiness right now. I just wanted to go home, take a shower, and shut everyone completely out of my life right now. I just want to be left alone.

***

Tonight was a double date. We just wanted a place where we could just chill and relax, so we went to the Sugar Factory. Ever since I met Miguel, we've been hanging out just about non-stop.

Sometimes we will double date with Heather and Simeon, Heather's husband, or we will go out with Tamara and Joseph. I really liked Miguel. He is always so sweet and kind when we are together. Just the other day in the music room, he played a song that he wrote to me just the night before. It wasn't a long song because it wasn't finished. It was titled Mi Amor, which means My Love. My love of art is the same as his love for music. The art is how we connect to the world.

That's where we found our inner peace. I love when he talks about his life and his family in Columbia. He is planning a trip to see his family later this year for only just a few days; he invited me to come with him. I told him I would. Heather and Simeon will also be joining us as well.

"How does your burger taste?" Simeon asked me.

"It's really good. It's juicy and the bread is soft. Do you like your fish tacos?"

"Yes, they're good! I'm trying to make room for dessert." He replied.

"We can take our dessert to go baby," Heather said to Simeon.

I laughed. "If y'all order a dessert to go, then I will take some home too."

"Maybe we can share a dessert," Miguel suggested.

"Maybe." I chuckled slyly, although, I don't think he was talking in a literal sense of eating food. "You are something else, Miguel."

"What?!" He laughed. "I was only talking about food. And if it goes beyond that, we shall see."

I felt his hand grab mine and bring it to his mouth to kiss it.

The rest of the time there we were laughing and enjoying each other's company. The food was amazing, and I even enjoyed the cookie-blasted chocolate milkshake. I couldn't finish all of it, so I asked for a cup to go. On the way home, Miguel sat close to me with his hand locked into mine. I was nervous. Besides Seth, I've never been with anyone else, and this was all too new for me. I felt Miguel lean closer to me.

"I really like you a lot" he whispered in my ear. "I think you're beautiful."

"You haven't seen me," I jokingly said to him.

"Yes, I have..."

He let go of my hand. I felt his hands touch my face, and then he pulled my face toward his and kissed me. It was warm and soft. I drifted into the caress of his lips, moving against mine. And here I am, sitting in the car, completely lost within a kiss. But no, I didn't stir away from it! I eagerly thirsted for more.

CHAPTER 17

I was pulling up over to JP's house. I left Sam back home. He's been quite the companion lately. He's been lying underneath me ever since I've been home. It's funny because the last few days I've been sad and depressed about my situation with Chelsea. When I lay on the couch thinking and shedding tears, Sam would come to me and make a whimpering sound. Then I would pat him and tell I'm ok. I think pets can read off our emotions. Sometimes, when I catch a quick glimpse of Sam, he looks like the spitting image of Elijah.

I missed my old friend.

It's true when they say cherish the elderly because they are so full of wisdom. And that's because God shares his wisdom through them. Getting old is not only a blessing that we live to see the many years given; it's the blessing of growing with an abundance of wisdom…one of God's many treasures. *If* we treasure it according to his will, of course. Wisdom grows with age. Although, it was a short period with Elijah, I felt like I've known him all my life.

I walked to the porch and rang the doorbell. I didn't tell JP that I was coming home from London. I wanted it to be a surprise for him. Lizzy opened the door and, to my surprise, had a baby draped over her shoulders.

She screamed in excitement. "Ah! JP!" The baby began to wail.

She rushed up to me and gave me a big hug.

"Hey!" as I hugged her back.

"I can't believe it!" she said still cradling the baby.

"What?!" I heard him approaching. "I almost broke my baby toe coming over here." he looked at me. "Seth! Ha-ha!" He came out the door and we hugged.

"You coming up in here looking like Grandpa Moses! I like your beard!" he pointed out. "How was London man?"

"It was great! I loved it!" I replied.

"Well, don't come up in here asking for tea, we only have some Cognac on the rocks here!" We all laughed.

"Look at you, you done lost some extra weight!"

"Whatever man! I'm still the same size!" I chuckled. "I see y'all have extended the family."

"That was Lizzy's doing. She trapped me, bro!"

"You need to stop! You kept crying and saying how much you wanted to have another baby," Lizzy responded. "If anything, *you* trapped me!"

"Ssh! Ssh! Baby, you can't tell my best friend how sensitive I am in the bedroom!"

"Hey, I can tell him more than that if he has time!"

I laughed again. "I do actually, but I want to hold him first."

"Yes, go to Uncle Seth so we can have a few hours of sleep!" JP said as Lizzy placed the baby in my arms. "Uncle Seth meet Austin."

Austin was fast asleep in my arms. He was super cute.

"He's really cute man! I still can't believe it! Y'all have another baby."

"We ready for you to have one, so I can be called Uncle JP!"

"You will be a great dad, Seth." Lizzy added in. She walked out of the room.

"So, when did you get back?" JP asked.

"It's been over a week now. I've been catching up and putting in applications."

"Do you think you will ever come back to the *Majestic*?"

"Nah! I want to do something completely new."

"So how was traveling around the world?"

I told JP about the whole adventure I had traveling to beautiful countries. I told him all of what I'd seen and the wonderful people that I met and encountered. I told him about Sam, Paul, and Elijah. I also told him about the incident that took place where I almost lost my life. In between the conversation, Lizzy came and took Austin because it was time for a change and feed. I also told him about future projects that I want to embark on to share my journey with the world.

"I'm glad you went. You seem like a whole different person sitting in front of me right now. That's a good thing. I'm proud of you bro!"

"Thanks, man!"

"So besides being home and looking for jobs, how is Chelsea doing? How did she react when you came back?"

"She hasn't reacted yet. I um...I haven't heard from her in a couple of years. You know, after I initially left, I sent a letter to her apologizing and everything. She responded back and we were talking for a moment. Then she went ghost. I asked if she wanted me to come back-that I *would* do that. And...*nothing!* I haven't heard from her since."

"Wow!" JP whispered.

"And to top that-I went to her place after I left the airport, and she's gone! *Gone bro!* The house was completely demolished!"

"What do you think?"

I shook my head, "I really don't know what to think."

"Maybe something happened that you don't know about. I'm sure if you talk to her you will know."

"*How?! I don't know where she is!*" I exclaimed. "*If she cared just a tinge about me-I would know!*"

"Hey man, I'm just trying to help," JP lift his hand defensibly, "You went way across the world, it's not like she can ride down the street to come see you. I'm just saying- *don't* give up too quickly. Just talk to her before you throw in the towel."

I sighed. "I don't know man. I love her deeply, but I'm just...hurt."

"Hey, sometimes wrongful acts bring consequences. Some light, some drastic. But we just have to deal with it and move forward bro." He placed his hand on my shoulder, "Sometimes we *expect* so much but don't *respect* the little. Just talk to her man."

I nodded.

"Hey, do you want to go to a jazz concert with us this weekend? We have a few extra tickets. There will be a lot of performers going on that night."

"Sure, I will go."

***

I was heading back to Chattanooga. I didn't have any plans for what I was going to do. I just felt like I needed to go there. I was up half the night thinking what my next move would be with

210

Chelsea and Chattanooga sprung into my mind. It was her home. And from our last visit, I loved how Chattanooga looked. The views of the city are spot on. Today was a bit cloudy with a little humidity outside. I just hope it doesn't rain. The only way that I could reach out to Chelsea was to talk to her family.

***

Kyla was running around the house playing with a few of her toys. I was on the couch listening to the music Tamara had on. I was already in the process of crocheting a blanket I was going to make for the baby. Even though Kobi is well over one year old, I still consider him a baby. It was still in the early part of noon, and I didn't have anything planned for today except stopping by the studio. I wanted to make sure everything was set to go for the art show that I am getting ready to prep for in the next couple of weeks. I have been super busy getting paintings together for the event. So busy that I decided to give myself a little break today. I should have been finished with this blanket months ago, but never had the extra time to complete it. I've barely even been at home; I've been spending the majority of my time with Miguel.

The phone rang.

Tamara walked into the living room.

"It's for you." She grabbed my hand and placed the phone in it.

"Hello."

"Hello Mi Amor." It was Miguel.

I got up from the couch to head towards my bedroom. "Hey Miguel! What are you doing?" I asked.

"I'm over my Uncle Ricardo's house." Miguel was always at his uncle's house. His uncle has the same love for music like Miguel. I believe that's who Miguel initially got inspiration from. His family was very nice and welcoming. Some moments it's hard for me to understand their dialect, but when I do, Miguel always whispers what was said. "Do you want to grab some dinner with later on?"

"Sure, I would love too."

"I will pick you up around six."

"That will be nice."

"Maybe later, we can go grab a movie. Or grab a show somewhere to listen to some music. I can have Heather grab some tickets with us if you would like that."

"Yes, we can go listen to a show tonight. I heard on the radio that Maxwell was performing this week. I love his music."

"Me too! Anything you want to do, we will go out to do it, okay senorita!" I heard a familiar footstep creep into my room.

"Miguel-I..." I whispered.

"Si."

"Gracious, te vere esta noche."

He laughed. "I am rubbing off on you quickly."

"Pequena." I laughed back. "I still have a lot of learning to do."

"Ok love, I will pick you up in a few."

"Okay, I'll see you then." I hung up the phone. "You don't have to sneak quietly into my room, you know. My conversation doesn't have to be discreet if you don't want it to be."

"I wasn't *trying* to listen to your conversation; I was just a little concerned-"

"*Concerned* about what?! Miguel and I are doing just fine. I don't need you butting in my life right now."

"I'm not *butting* in. I just don't see my cousin as much as I used to. This relationship is going really fast, and I just don't want you to settle for someone *just* because, you know."

"I'm *not* settling-Miguel is a great guy!"

"I'm not saying he isn't a good guy Chelsea, I'm just saying that-"

"He asked me to marry him…" I blurted.

The room fell silent.

"And I said yes" I whispered. I was lost in the response I gave her. I stood there thinking on the word, 'yes'.

"Do you love him?"

The question sat there right in my mind.

"Do you love him, Chelsea?"

"I can learn to love him. He is such a sweet person." Tears began to swell in my eyes. I heard Tamara walking closely to me.

"What about Seth?"

"What about him?" I retorted back to her. Even as harsh as I sounded, I didn't intend to be. I was still hurting. "I mean-I can't wait forever. He's probably moved on himself. I *can't* put things on hold for him when another opportunity is there." I shook my head, "I can't do that!"

"I'm not asking you to. It's your life, your decisions." She placed a hand on my shoulder. "It just wouldn't be right for me to sit around and not say anything. *I* just can't do that. And I *know* you still love Seth. And I may be selfish because I don't want my cousin to run off and leave me."

"Yep, that's it!" I chuckled to myself.

"Yeah, but what I do know is...loves at *best* when we wait."

"Oh, yeah?" The annoyance was beginning to filter.

"Mm-hmm!" she replied as her footsteps walked away from me,

"Love can sometimes make us wait."

And I stood there, playing those words in my mind.

***

I reached into my pocket to pull out a toy dinosaur and placed it on Chase's tombstone. I laid a bundle of roses each upon Mr. and Mrs. Davis tombstones as well. I stood there looking with my hands in my pocket. I felt like family this second time around then just a stranger. Strangely enough, it was a bit humid on the way here, but standing here, I felt a bit of a breeze. I know right now this is the place I needed to be at the moment. I don't know why but I *had* to be here.

"I don't know what I'm supposed to say. I just wished the circumstances were different. I would have loved just waiting for the moment to meet you all. Of course, I would have been a bit nervous... but I *think* y'all would have liked me." I chuckled to myself. "I can be a bit stubborn at times, though I'm sure my brother and sister would testify to that. But I consider myself a pretty decent guy. I think you would have put me under your wing, Mr. Davis." The back of my throat tightened and I wiped a tear that was forming in the corner of my inner eyes. "Sir, I love your daughter. And I promise to take care of her like you once did. She truly misses you guys. And I miss her beyond words. I hope

God will show me the way...back to her heart."

Just then a bird swoops down on top of Mrs. Davis's tomb-stone. It looked around for a brief second. Then the bird flew back off into the sky. I smiled as I watched it fly away.

***

The jazz concert was really nice. Heather's husband, Simeon, got us close up, sitting near the stage. I didn't know where the stage was exactly located, but from where we were sitting, the music was loud. Heather said that the show was sold out. We had to get there an extra hour earlier so that the workers could usher us toward the handicapped section of the room. The area where we were wasn't a long distance from the entrance building, because we didn't have to walk very far to get to our seats. The sound of the music and voices seemed to echo the room pretty much, so the room had to be large. I was glad when Miguel invited me to come to the concert with him. I love to listen to music. Music helps me with my art in a lot of ways. It helps expand my mind to creativity. Music can make you sing, dance, or think.

I don't know how many performers there were that performed, but it seemed like a lot. I really enjoyed myself. I can tell Miguel did because he would sing right along with the sound of instru-ments. I could feel the rhythm of his leg bumping against mine. He held onto my hand the whole night of the concert.

There were times I felt he was trying to make conversation with me, but the blare of the music was too loud for me to hear him. Or at least that's what I kept trying to tell myself. I wasn't too up for conversation tonight. I just needed to get out of the house tonight. Tamara's words still lingered in my mind... *Do you love him?*

Love means waiting...

215

I know you love Seth...

I can feel the sweat of my hands locked into Miguel's. I know if I felt it, I'm sure that he felt it too, but he didn't let on to me that he did. I *never* thought I would be the one deciding on which man would be better for me.

Me?!

The show was over, and we were heading out of the building. It took a moment because there were a lot of people there. Heather was on my left shoulder, guiding my arm out of the building. The night air was a bit cool and there was a breeze.

"Whew! The wind is a bit nippy!" I said.

"We are just a couple of steps to the car," Heather replied. "Yes, we have to crank up the heat! I'm getting cold. Ok, watch your step here on the sidewalk. Simeon didn't park too close by it, so you will have to step down."

"Ok." I replied.

Just then, the wind picked up, and I caught a whiff of a smell.

A familiar smell that hung in my nose...peppermint and musk. *Seth!*

I jerk my head to the direction of the smell. My heart sank deep within my body. My breath hung right there in my lungs. I couldn't move!

It's him! His scent! Seth is here!

"Chelsea?! Are you okay?!" I heard the concern in Heather's voice. I moved a couple of steps toward the smell.

"Mi amor!?" Miguel echoed from behind.

"Chelsea?! Your shaking-are you okay?" I felt her hand tightened around my arm. She stopped my movement.

No, I'm not, ok?! I wanted to scream out. *I know he's here.*

"We have to go now." Heather pulled back on my arm.

"Y-Y-Yes." I stammered in a whisper. Heather led me back into the car, but I was still watching the area of that familiar smell...the smell that had once captured me. And all I could think about was...

Seth is home.

CHAPTER 18

She knew I was there.

I was lying on the couch with Sam right beside me as I rubbed his neck. I kept replaying the moment when I saw Chelsea and when she noticed I was there. I first saw her in the hallway as she was walking toward the exit sign. She was holding hands with a Latin fellow I'd never seen before. She looked pretty. She had on a long sparkling silver dress with her hair tied up in a ponytail. I was standing there with JP when I spotted her. I followed her out until she drove away. I made sure to keep my distance. I wanted to speak to her, but I just couldn't. I guess it was the fear of not knowing what to say that held me back. Even though my heart was a bit broken before, it's definitely on ten now because she has moved on to someone else.

Being hurt hurts like hell

Even though I don't know what hell feels like and never have any intention to know what it feels like. Being hurt feels like the deepest part of your soul is aching.

Now I sit here second-guessing myself if I ever should have even come home in the first place. Or I never should have left home in the beginning. It never occurred to me that she would have moved on so quickly like that.

Did she ever love me? I thought to myself. Was forgiving me her last resolution toward finding happiness in someone else?

I looked at Sam who was looking dead at me. He looked just as sad as I did.

"I'm sorry boy," I gently rubbed on him, "I'm just a little sad today."

He made a light whimper and then barked. Then he looked up and hopped down from the couch. I lifted from the couch as he disappeared from the living room. A moment later he returns with my journal in his mouth.

Oh, man! Sam touched me at that moment. He found the one thing I loved to do that would help cheer me up.

"Thanks, boy!" I rubbed behind his ears, and he licked me.

I didn't know if I was ready to start writing in my journal today. I honestly felt like simply resting. I was physically drained emotionally.

My cell phone rings.

"Hello?"

"Yes, may I speak with a Mr. Seth Calloway?" a female voice asked.

"Yes, I'm Seth."

"Great! My name is Deanna Walters. I'm the secretary for Lucas Thomason here at Atlanta Global Times Free Press. We've been interviewing a lot of potential candidates for the marketing editor position that you applied for."

"Yes."

"Mr. Thomason has a busy schedule for the next couple of weeks. If possible, he would like to set up an interview with you today. Do you think you will be able to come in today for an interview?"

"Of course! I can come in anytime today-whatever is convenient for Mr. Thomason."

"Ok, great! How about four o'clock this afternoon?"

"That works for me!"

"Ok, if you have a pencil and paper I can give you the address."

"Yes-just one moment…"

I looked around the living room but didn't see anything. I dashed into the room and hit my elbow against the door frame. The painful sensation flared through my arm. I quickly grabbed a pen from my nightstand and a billing statement that was on top.

"Ok, I'm ready."

She gave me the address of the building and also informed me that there would be free parking across the lot. As soon as I arrive, I will have to check in downstairs and then head up to the fourth floor. I hung up the phone and sat on the bed. The jolt of pain still lingered in my arm, but I could overlook that. All I can think about is this job interview. I am super excited about this one.

Atlanta Global Times Press is the largest newspaper in the metropolitan state of Georgia. This is even bigger than my previous job The Majestic. This will definitely open up doors for me because Global is where I want to be right now. Sam came into my bedroom.

"Come here, boy." Sam walked to me, and I rubbed his coat. Then he started licking my face. "I have an interview today. I want you to send up some puppy prayers for me, okay? Come on, let's go for a walk."

After the walk, I got myself showered and dressed for the interview. I still had some time to kill so I stopped by Walgreens to pick up some vitamins and gum. I had to go down the aisles to find what I was looking for because this Walgreens I've never been to.

It was built a couple of years ago, but it's close to my interview site. I still was walking around checking out the items in the store when I turned the aisle and spotted Kristy! Our eyes locked on each other. I haven't seen her since the incident at Chelsea's house. She'd called a few times after the incident, but I never answered. I know JP and Lizzy had stopped hanging around her. She looked completely different. She looks like the past couple of years have worn her. She looked tired. I looked over to the side of her, and there, right beside was a little boy about two to three years old. I looked back at Kristy and noticed that she was pregnant again.

"Hey, Seth!"

"Hey."

"I'm so surprised to see you! I thought someone told me that you moved out of the country."

"I did! But it was only short-lived. I recently moved back a couple of months ago. I see you've been busy."

"Yes, this is Quinton. And I have one that's coming due soon."

"Wow! Congratulations to you and your family! Are you married now?"

"No, but I'm sure I will be pretty soon."

I looked at Quinton. I wanted to see if he resembled me in any way.

"Don't worry Seth, he's not yours," Kristy said.

"Are you sure?" I asked. "I want you to be certain about this."

"I'm sure! Besides if he was, he doesn't need you anyway. He's had a dad ever since he's been born. Remember you were the one who left us."

"I was never with you in the first place Kristy! You took advantage of me and the whole situation! I never wanted you period!"

"It's funny because you didn't stop me that night. You enjoyed every bit of it."

"I want a paternity test."

"Like I said, he's not yours. And your blind friend will never come near him! Come on Quinton!" She walked away from me.

I'm going to get that test done regardless of what she said. If anything, I want to make sure. And if he is mine, I'm damn sure going to fight for him.

***

"You have a great portfolio here. I've read a lot of your columns before. I absolutely loved them.

You have a great talent there Mr. Calloway. The Majestic is a great company to work for. Why did you decide that you no longer want to work there?"

"Mr. Thomason, I felt like I was in a box, and everything was uniform to what my boss wanted. It was hard to find a creative box there to expand to a broader spectrum with trends, fashion, and styles. I want to do more than just that. I want to talk about more relatable issues and be able to network more globally." Mr. Thomason nodded taking every word in that I said.

"The past few years of me traveling from country to country has shown me how much we negate that natural, organic origin of what America used to be before technology took over. I'm not saying that technology is bad because it's not. Just seeing other places of the world makes you appreciate culture. There's history amongst every culture that's hidden or unknown. Sometimes even neglected or erased. I want to talk about the real stuff. I met a woman who planted spices in her garden and created her own spice, which became a popular name in the town. Seeing all of that motivates me to see what we can do here."

"That's the attitude I am looking for to be on my team. I feel like you will be a great asset to this company. And I would love for you to share your ideas. Creativity is what helps my company to thrive. How about being the chief marketing director for my paper and magazine?"

"Magazine?!"

"Yes, we've expanded, and we would like to market a magazine as well. I want you to be the publisher. You'll be able to share what you learned from your travels as well as what you put out locally. You can title the column however you like."

"Wow! Thank you, Mr. Thomason!"

"No, thank you! We need someone like you here. I have a feeling you're going to teach us some great things."

"Will I have a team to work for?"

"Yes, you can put your own team together."

"Thanks, I have a couple of people whom I like to bring over from the Majestic. They're a talented bunch who will bring success over to the newspaper as well."

"Hey as long as they keep the environment positive, I don't mind at all."

"Yes Mr. Thomason they will."

"Also let them know that this isn't always a sit-down office type of job. They will have to travel with you when I send you out."

"Oh, I'm sure that they will be all for that, sir."

"Ok, we will see you next week. Of course, if they need to work out a notice we will work with them on that."

"Ok, we will see you next week. I thank you, Mr. Thomason, for the opportunity to work for your company. It means a lot." He got up to shake my hand.

"No, I thank you for wanting to take part in our family here. Hey, if you don't have any plans this week, that will be an art show at a studio called Miracle Art. I have a few extra tickets left. There's this amazing artist who's blind whose paintings are every bit beautiful. It would be amazing to know just how she does it.

You more than welcome to come."

"I would love to go!"

***

I decided that going to the art studio would be a great idea to see Chelsea again. I didn't know if I was going to say something to her. I wanted to, but I just wanted to see how things were going to play out. The night air was still cool. I decided to wear a nice black suit. I'm glad Mr. Thomason had some extra tickets to spare. I'm sure it's going to be a packed event. It's funny how I was at my lowest point emotionally when I received a call, went to an interview, and landed the position. God is indeed good. I really needed a job, and I believe this job will open up doors for me in all aspects. I told JP that I wanted him to come over to join the team, and he was on board about the whole thing. Jacob took a little bit more convincing; he had gotten a promotion so he was undecided about what to do. But in the end, he loved working together and thought this would better advance his career than the Majestic. I couldn't wait to begin this next chapter in my life.

I pulled up to the gallery and it was really packed. A lot of the time was spent looking for a parking space. I had to settle with parking around the corner and walked to the studio. When I walked inside the entrance, I was completely blown away by how everything looked. The studio was a two-story building with portraits lined on every single wall. I tried to squeeze by the crowd near the entrance, but it was still just as crowded on the inside. I looked around but didn't spot Chelsea anywhere. I began to walk around the lower level on the main floor looking at the portraits. There were a couple of paintings I noticed before that were hung in her room, but for the most part, these paintings were all new to me. Eventually, ushers came to guide us back into the main room. On top of the stairs, Mr. Chaplin introduced everyone to Chelsea as she made her entrance to join him on top. She was led by the same woman I saw at the concert. The man who was holding her hand was escorted as well. He must be blind also. I thought to myself. She seemed happy. The guy standing beside her is all smiles.

I saw him touch her arm and lock his hands with her.

I saw it!

I saw a ring on her finger She is engaged! No!

I had to make sure. I walked in between people to get a closer look at her finger. I tried not to get as close, as I walked up the stairs. The closer I got, the more vivid it became. I realized I lost her.

CHAPTER 19

School felt like it lasted forever today. The kids were fussier today than in the previous sections that I taught the last couple of weeks. I was teaching the class how to papier-mâché a Styrofoam circular ball that was donated by an organization. We actually received a lot of art tools and supplies from them, and it really helped out tremendously. I asked Mr. Weber if he could come in to help me with the class as I taught them how to papier-mâché. I don't know what caused the children to be extremely active today, but I was glad that Mr. Weber was there to intervene and help. I've been a little overwhelmed lately with school, the studio, and my personal life. I haven't had any extra free time to get back into my own paintings. So, I decided I needed to cut back on some things that are going on right now. I talked with Dr. Hill, who was head of the blind school, about cutting down my schedule a bit. I will only work on Mondays and Wednesdays just the morning sessions. I needed to work more on my paintings as well as help Mr. Chaplin at our studio. Dr. Hill agreed that it would be fine and I told her I would finish the rest of this term as is. I just needed a better healthy balance in my life right then.

After class was over, Mr. Weber escorted the kids back to their classes and came back to help me clean up the room. We talked and laughed about the kids' behavior in the class. Mr. Weber said that after today, he was in dire need of going on a vacation. I told him we both needed to even if it was only a staycation. As we exited and locked up the classroom, I had music playing from down the hallway. I knew it was time to talk to Miguel. I have been avoiding the issue by not returning his calls for the past couple of days, but I couldn't hold out any longer.

I walked down the hallway. It felt like a long stretch even though it was a short distance.

I was a little nervous.

The last thing that I wanted to do was to break his heart. But I had to be honest with him as well as myself. I just *knew* I couldn't be with him. It was all just bad timing.

I made my way to the entrance of the music room. The song that he was playing on the piano sounds beautiful. I stood there listening as he stroked every key...the pureness of each sound rang heavily in my ears as I closed my eyes. He is truly a musician. He speaks through his music.

"Chelsea!" Heather announced loudly.

I smiled.

I heard her footsteps quickly approaching me. I felt her arms wrapped me in a hug.

"Where have you been?" she demanded. "You didn't come to your music lesson the other day, nor did you return my call."

"Yeah, I've been going through some personal things right now. But once everything settles, I will continue with your lessons."

"Oh," she said surprisingly, "I didn't realize that you were going through something. You take all the time you need ok. Is there anything I can do to help?"

"No, not at the moment. Thanks for offering."

"Anytime" she replied.

"Can you take me to Miguel? I need to talk with him for a moment."

"Sure" She took my arm and led me to the seat where Miguel was fiddling with some keys. She helped me on the piano bench so that I could talk with him. Then I heard her walk away.

"Hey, Miguel."

"Hello, Chelsea." I could hear the sadness in his voice.

"I'm sorry I didn't return your calls the times that you called me. I've been thinking a lot about things...a lot about us."

"Really?" he said, excitement in his voice. "I thought you were upset about me. I had *no clue* what it was. You are fine now!"

"*Miguel!*" I paused. This was a lot tougher than I imagined. A lot! I began to feel water filter into my eyes.

"Yes senorita," he said calmly. It makes it worse when you hear his beautiful accent.

"Miguel, I can't marry you" I felt around the bench to touch his leg. "I think you're a wonderful, loving person. But my heart belongs to someone else. It *always* belonged to him."

"Why didn't you ever mention it to me before? Why didn't you say anything?"

"I don't know, I think because you filled an empty void in my life. Then it all went so fast that I just *went* with it. And I wanted to learn to love you as you love me, but I couldn't do that. I had to be honest with myself and you because I *do like you,* Miguel."

"I like you too."

"Maybe things would have been different if I would have met you first. Then maybe things could turn out a little differently. Or may not, I don't know."

"That's a lot of maybes. If a relationship was built on maybes, then it would have never worked out in the first place. I'm glad you told me now and then later. I don't know how I would have taken it if you told me at the altar."

I chuckled. "I would have never done you like that. You're too special to me."

"I would have been a great husband to you."

"I know." I gently took the ring from my finger. I felt for his arm until I reached his hand and placed the ring in it. "One day you'll find love again and she will return the love *willingly.*"

"I hope so, and to you as well."

"He will." I got up from my seat. "I hope we still get to play together. I would love that."

"Si Senorita, me too"

I left the piano bench and walked back the way I came. Heather grabbed my arm to lead me back out of the music room. That was the hardest thing that I had to do, even harder than having to learn how to be blind. I didn't want to hurt him or anyone for that matter. I know he will find that one special person that he's meant to be with. As I was walking out, Miguel strummed the keys hard and then began to play some music. It wasn't the happy, cheerful music that he normally played. It was sad...so sad... but beautiful.

***

Today was a fun day to hang out with the family. After we left the morning service at church, we decided to have a picnic lunch in the park. It was a sunshine day and Kyla wanted to get out on her bike. I decided to bring a painting pad, my brushes, and tubes of paint to sketch a painting. It's been a long time since I've been to a park and I wanted to make the most of it. We set up our blanket right under a big tree to get some shade. Tamara packed some sandwiches, a canteen of chicken noodle soup, chips, fruit, and banana pudding for dessert. Joseph was with Kyla helping her ride her bike. I can hear baby Kobi babbling with his toys. I can hear Tamara setting the dishes on the blanket.

"I got off the phone with Mama, and she is heading toward us. She said she hasn't picnic in a while, so she wanted to come."

"I think she came because you mentioned that you made banana pudding." I laughed, "Anytime you make banana pudding, your mom always drops by to pick up a plate."

"I'm glad it's not as hot as today like it was yesterday. Then we would have had an indoor picnic."

"Me too! It has a nice cool breeze. I'm loving it!"

"Do you think I should have brought watermelon?" She asked me.

"Um- why didn't you ask the question?"

"Next time we have a picnic, I'm going to bring some watermelon."

"Yes, watermelon and cantaloupe."

Tamara laughed, "I've never heard someone say bring cantaloupe on a picnic. Watermelon-yes! Cantaloupe-no!"

"Well, I will seriously tear up some cantaloupe! Sprinkle a little honey on top! You don't know what you're missing!"

"What the world?" Tamara loudly shrieked.

"What is it?!" I asked.

"Your girl is here."

"Who?!"

"Kristy...and she's not alone."

"What? Who's with her?" I asked but the irritation was displayed in my voice.

"No, it's not Seth. She is with some guy and a little boy. She is also pregnant."

"Wow! I wasn't expecting that. Does she see us?"

"I don't know but eventually she will because they are sitting right across the way from us."

"Well, I'm glad she has finally moved on. I can't believe she has a child and another one on the way. Do you think it's Seth?"

"It's hard to tell from way over here. It could be you know. The person who she is with seems like he could be quite a handful. She looks different now."

"Maybe it's the pregnancy."

"No, it looks like karma!" Tamara implied.

"You need to stop. Maybe she's in a better place right now."

"If only you can see this. As long as she doesn't start any mess- we good! Let me get our plates together. We have plenty of food."

I continued my painting wondering if Seth is indeed a dad now.

I wonder if knows or not. I thought to myself. *I just can't believe it.*

My thoughts were interrupted by Kyla talking about her bike ride.

"Did you see me mama? Daddy took me on a big hill, and I was going super-fast!"

"Did he now?"

"The hill wasn't too big baby. She did really good though." I heard him give her a smooch. Kobi began to wail.

"Hey, what's the matter, little man?" Joseph said, "Pretty soon, you'll be riding on a bike, too."

"He's probably ready to eat. Let me feed him right quick. If y'all ready to eat, you can fix your plate."

I heard her pick Kobi up because his crying stopped.

"After I fix Kyla's plate, I'll fix your plate, Chelsea," Joseph said to me.

"I'm not hungry now. I will eat in a bit."

"Are you all, right?"

"We have some company across the way we weren't expecting," Tamara interjected.

"Who?" he asked.

"Kristy," I answered. "Apparently, she has a kid and one on the way."

All at once there was a loud commotion heard from where we were sitting. I heard a guy yelling and a woman screaming back at him.

"What the world?" Tamara said, "Now they are extremely loud. And he is just cussing her out!"

He was loud. All I could hear was F-this and F-that. And if she was hungry, get her other pimps to pay for her food. I can hear a child crying.

"I'm about to go over there to help diffuse the situation," Joseph said.

"No, you're not! We don't know anything about him. He might have a weapon!" said Tamara.

"He doesn't look like it. Besides he's walking away. Let me check on them right quick."

"I want to go with you," I said.

"You sure?!"

"Yes."

Joseph took my arm and led me across the way with him. As we got closer, I could hear the child whimpering a bit.

"Are you okay?" Joseph asked.

"Yeah, I'm f-," She must have spotted me. "I'm fine. I'm just waiting for my ride to pick me up."

"You can sit with us while you wait. We have plenty of food if you are hungry." I added.

"No. We're fine. We don't need your help." she snapped at me.

"Hungry" the child repeated.

"Yes, do you want to come over and get something to eat?" I said to the child.

"*I said we're fine!*" she got loud.

"Look, this doesn't have anything to do with me or you! This is a child that's hungry-your child."

"And Seth's." she reminds me coyly.

"Either way, we have plenty of food. Come on." I reached out my hand, and seconds later, a small hand joined mine. Joseph led us back to the picnic area.

Kristy eventually came and joined us. I could smell her presence nearby. She didn't say anything the whole time she was sitting there. Tamara told me later that her son enjoyed the food, and that Kristy helped herself to a plate as well. They may have stayed about thirty minutes and left. Even though she's not at the top of my list of favorite people in the world, I still wanted to show her that even in the midst of being mean, I still wanted to show her kindness. I *had* to show her that! Even though it wasn't easy at first, I felt good in the end. Because sometimes people *want* to see you at your lowest in order for them to feel good about themselves when they do you wrong. But an act of kindness can make all the difference in the world.

CHAPTER 20

Months later

I was finished with my book. I have already taken it to a publisher to get everything started to print. I was excited. I've written columns, articles, and short stories, but I never would have imagined myself publishing a whole book. I enjoyed every moment of putting this book together. I was at Starbucks purchasing a frappe before I headed to the park with Sam. Days like this make me miss living in London and working at the shop. I called Paul a couple of days ago to check on him and his family. He said that he was back to his normal self and the shop was still busier than ever. He talked about coming out here to see me in September when the flights were cheaper.

It would be great for me to start planning on things we could do together when he and his family come to visit. It will be as if I never left London. He said he was going to bring me a big supply of his tea since mine is going low. I told him if he comes here, he may never want to go back, and I will look at some vacation homes just in case he does decide to stay a little longer.

He was all for that.

The park wasn't as busy as it normally was in the early afternoon. People come to the park on their lunch break or dog walkers on their scheduled routine around the same time. The park usually has more movement than it does today. I decided I wanted to play fetch with Sam, so I brought his favorite ball to toss around. Sam's busy body was going a mile a minute. After thirty minutes or so, we went to the bench to rest. Sam was lying right beneath my feet. Sitting there, I started to reminisce about the times I had enjoyed my company with Elijah. I really do miss him. I remember him taking me to the Tower Bridge and showing me a stone that had his great-great father's initials there. I think Elijah lost himself not only in the death of his sister but in the depth of the Great Depression that his family had suffered. His parents had worked day in and day out for only just about a small amount of change that barely supported them. Poverty and grief had stricken him deeply. He wore that heavily on his back for years, never once living to let it all go. Well, maybe I helped him let it go a little bit. I saw a change in him just before he died. He was no longer the Elijah I met at the beginning. With Sam beside me, I could still feel his presence. In the book I wrote, I had to share Elijah's journey in life. In my stories and articles, I have to tell people stories to the world to create something better. I understand now what Elijah was trying to convey to me. Use my gift of writing to help create a better history for tomorrow.

I got up to go home.

I now have to come up with some ideas for a great title for my column. Instead of walking to the car, I thought jogging would be better.

And so, did Sam.

***

Work was steady today. I had a couple of meetings today. One was meeting with the team to discuss what will be put into the first issue of our magazine pages. Even though we are still part of the newspaper Global Life, he wanted me to headline the magazine.

We decided to title the magazine Global Era. A title like this can feature a lot of things and expand in a lot of areas and trends. A better tomorrow can be for our health, fashion, trends, living, travel, finance, religion, and many more. It's going to be a magazine where people can share their content and creations with the world. I will also have a personal column that I will produce, but I haven't found a title for that just as yet.

JP and I were working in my office trying to pull the creative side of the magazine together.

"I think it is going to be a great contender for a good magazine, especially in the Atlanta region. Maybe even the whole southeastern region." JP said.

"Yeah, I agree with you. This magazine will hit people on a more personal level. And that's what people like to see and read."

"Yeah, they do." He begins to tap his pencil on the table. "So um, what were the results?"

"I haven't looked at it just yet."

"Man, what are you waiting for?!" he shrieked. "You went through all this legal work to find out whether this child is yours or not! Where's the result? Let me look at bro!"

I pulled the envelope from the top drawer of my desk.

"I received it earlier today. I don't know. Part of me wants to know man and the other part of me, I don't. Maybe I can still be like a father figure to him regardless. JP if only you would have seen his little face."

"You have baby fever, bro!" He looked at me with a concern face-his silly concerned face. "I want to know because I might be an uncle. Besides, if he's not, then there are no ties to Kristy. You can start your own family."

I laughed. Silly JP. "You're already an uncle."

"Yeah, but not by you."

I tore up the envelope and pulled out the letter. I began to read the results. I was speechless. I was still reading it over and over, 99.9999999 percent.

"So, what does it say?" JP urged.

"It says I'm not the father," I answered. "He doesn't belong to me."

"Whew, I know that was a bit of relief. Are you okay?"

"Yeah." I was still looking at the results. "Part of me would have been open to becoming a dad. I do want to start a family one day."

"Yeah, I hear ya. But now it can be done the right way bro-with someone you love."

"Yeah, you're right."

Mrs. Thomason knocked on the door and came in.

"I'm just going around letting people know of the construction that's about to take place."

"What construction?" JP asked.

"A wall is going to be torn down to expand some more offices to provide better workspace and opportunities for more employment."

He was starting to walk out of the office. A thought crossed my mind. "Mr. Thomason, do you know who is contracting this job?"

"Yep, it's Joseph Constructions. We use him all the time. He does great work."

"Thanks"

Mr. Thomason walked out, and JP turned to look at me. "Hey, what was that all about?"

"Fate."

I told JP to continue working and I will be right back.

***

It was a Saturday afternoon. Tamara had decided to host a cookout and bring some of the family here at the house. My Aunt Vi, Tamara's mom, and Uncle Frank, Tamara's dad, were all seated at the table. Our cousins, Courtney, Robert, Zoe, and Lamar came to the outing as well. It's been a while since we had a cookout. We used to try to do it every couple of months, but that did plan out so well. People have lives and other obligations to attend to. Joseph put some chicken, shrimp, corn, and steaks on the grill. Tamara cooked some baked beans, potato salad, greens, and cornbread muffins to go with the meat. Aunt Vi brought over some sherbet ice cream and a homemade pound cake. There were a few kids running around the house as well. I sat at the table listening to their stories and laughing at their jokes. It felt so good being around family.

I've been getting myself together. Work was beginning to become organized and well-balanced. I recently sold two paintings and made a very substantial amount of money. I donate a supplement of that to the blind school. The school needs some repairs and up-to-date equipment and supplies. My life was beginning to become normalized now. Everything was happening so fast, and I was a bit overwhelmed. But now I'm back at a pace that was familiar. There was a knock on the door.

"I'll get it!" I heard Tamara's footsteps coming from the kitchen. It must be another family member that Tamara invited. I got up from the table and began walking to get another scoop of ice cream in my bowl.

"Ooh, who are you?" Aunt Vi asked as if she had forgotten she had a husband.

"Hello, Chelsea." The smooth sound of his voice sent a shock wave that rippled through my body. The bowl from my hand slipped right through my fingers and crashed on the floor.

"Seth?!" I whispered as if my breath was completely knocked out of me.

"I'll pick this bowl up," Tamara said.

"Why are you here?" I asked him.

"Well, Joseph and Tamara invited me. And I'm glad that they did."

"Yeah?"

"Mm-hmm. Can I talk to you privately?"

"We can go out to the patio."

I led him to the chairs outside. Once outside I sat down in my normal chair, and I felt him sit beside me.

"So how have you been doing?" he asked.

"I have been ok-just work, school, and the studio. I've sold a couple of paintings recently. How about you?"

"I'm doing well! I work for the newspaper and now we've migrated to distributing magazines for the same company. I will be able to do columns and articles the way I would like them. It's been amazing."

"I'm so proud of Seth. You deserve it all."

"As you too. I meant every word that I've ever said to you." He grabbed my hand. "Chelsea, I finished my book."

"You did?!" I gleamed.

"Yes, and I wanted the first published book to go to you." I heard the familiar sound of his satchel being opened. He grabbed my hand and placed the book in it. "Go ahead and feel it."

I begin to feel around the book. "It's in Braille!" I started smiling and began feeling the title, Love Comes in Many Colors.

"I wanted you to be the first one to read it."

"Oh, Seth!" My eyes began to water, "Thank you."

"I want you to read the introduction."

I opened the book to feel the words written before the story,

Love brings new beginnings,
Love ties up old endings,
Love conquers our biggest regrets,
Love overcomes our deepest fears,
Love heals our sorrow and pain,
And Love creates a beautiful journey,
Chelsea, my love, come ride the waves with me.
-Seth Calloway

My hand went to the end of the period and over to a circular shape. *A ring!*

I couldn't believe it! I stood there completely voiceless with my hand over the ring. My body was completely overwhelmed with emotions...overwhelmed with happiness and joy. I was trying to speak-my mouth was moving but nothing came out. I felt his hand rubbed up and down my back.

"I can't finish *our* story without you!" He whispered to me.

"Oh, Seth!" Tears began to pour down my face. He placed the ring on my trembling finger.

"Chelsea, I've loved you since the first time I saw you. As I've gotten to know you, it only grew. And throughout my journey, you were always there to encourage me, you loved me, and most of all you forgave even when I hurt you the deepest."

"ELF," she whispered.

"What?"

"Encourage, Love, and Forgive means ELF," she chuckled. "You're Santa's little helper."

"Wow!" he laughed. "I guess I never thought of something like that. Hey, I guess I am! I'm an ELF. And so are you, babe."

"Yes, we are. But we're God's helpers too," she added.

"Indeed, we are."

"Chelsea, you haven't answered my question."

"And what's that?" I whispered to him.

"Will you marry me?" I felt his breath hollow against my face.

"I do Seth," smiling at him.

He pulled my face to his and kissed me deeply. I heard the cheers and screams from my family erupt from the patio door. And I felt the love erupt from the brink of my soul. I was happy. And I was ready to take on this new journey with him.

EPILOGUE

Christmas Day

I was at the table laughing at JP making a joke about the game he watched on TV the other day. Simeon was sitting across the way asking JP about the game of basketball. JP, Simeon, Paul, Joseph, and their families were here at our house. Chelsea and the wives were cooking and bringing out dishes to set on the table. The food smelled delightful, and I was ready to eat. The kids were all running around while the sweet sound of Christmas music played softly in the background. The house was filled with beautiful decorations with scented candles, the essence of the room. We were so excited to be hosting Christmas this year that I decided to put up an extra tree. Tree number six was sitting on top of the island in the kitchen. It was only a small tree though, but it was the prettiest. There were ornaments of angels that had my parents, Chelsea's parents, and brother's names engraved on them. We also had an angel for Elijah. It was so great to be around family. Life was great! Paul and his family were making frequent trips to see us, Chelsea and I were traveling a lot, and work was prosperous for both of us. Chelsea continued to paint and only volunteered at the school once a week. I looked up at her. We're only a couple of months away before the little one comes. Baby girl is already doing the most. Chelsea was rubbing her stomach.

"Daddy! Daddy!" Ella ran me. I grabbed her and placed her in my lap to give her a hug.

"What's wrong Ella?"

"Elijah won't share his toys with me?" she told me.

"Tell him twins are supposed to share. Y'all have the tightest bond than anyone on Earth!"

"Even tighter than Santa Daddy?!"

"Yes!" I laughed and kissed her cheek. "Even tighter than Santa!"

She threw her arms over me, kissed me on the cheek, and gave me a big hug. Chelsea came in carrying a bowl of rolls to put on the table.

"You're going to spoil her!"

"Yeah, I'm going to spoil all of my babies...including you!"

I got up and wrapped my arms around her waist and planted kisses on her neck. She was laughing.

"Stop it! We have company!"

"Hey, I'm just dancing with my baby." I started swaying my hips.

Just then Sam made a funny noise and looked toward the door. He sat there staring for a moment.

"What's the matter, Sam?" Chelsea asked.

I walked toward him.

"Maybe he needs to go potty," Chelsea said.

"I took him an hour ago," I replied, "Let me check it out." I walked toward the window and looked outside.

"Oh wow!" I cheered with excitement.

"What, babe?"

I turned to see Chelsea walking in my direction. "It's snowing outside!"

I opened the door, and Sam ran out in the yard. I walked out onto the porch. Everyone else followed right behind me talking and laughing about the snow. Simeon jumped off the porch to kick the snow and then did a snow angel. Elijah walked up and reached out to hold my hand.

"Daddy, can we go play in the snow?"

"Sure son, just get your coat, hat, and gloves?"

"Yay!" He took off to grab his things.

All the kids and adults were outside celebrating this day, this fellowship, and the snow. Snowballs were being thrown all over the place. I just remembered being a little boy playing in the snow with my family. Nothing like the good old days. Then I thought about my column for the magazine, "What's your Season" displayed in my mind. I love it! I finally found the heading for my column. That heading truly represents me, family, friends, neighbors, and culture. I looked over and saw Chelsea standing by the doorway. I went over to guide her on the porch.

"Is it beautiful, Seth?"

"Yes, it is sweetheart...but not as beautiful as you!" I kissed her under our mistletoe. I grabbed both her hands to guide her off the porch. "Now let's go play!"

Chelsea smiled.

The End